THE MANCHESTER MYSTERY

kaboom!

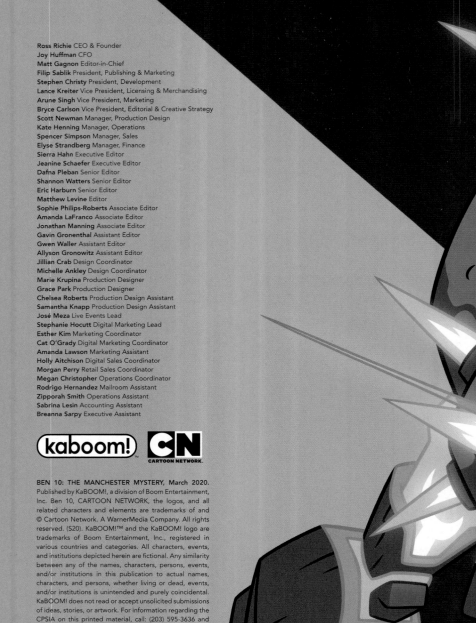

kaboom! | **CN** CARTOON NETWORK.

BEN 10: THE MANCHESTER MYSTERY, March 2020.
Published by KaBOOM!, a division of Boom Entertainment,
Inc. Ben 10, CARTOON NETWORK, the logos, and all
related characters and elements are trademarks of and
© Cartoon Network. A WarnerMedia Company. All rights
reserved. (S20). KaBOOM!™ and the KaBOOM! logo are
trademarks of Boom Entertainment, Inc., registered in
various countries and categories. All characters, events,
and institutions depicted herein are fictional. Any similarity
between any of the names, characters, persons, events,
and/or institutions in this publication to actual names,
characters, and persons, whether living or dead, events,
and/or institutions is unintended and purely coincidental.
KaBOOM! does not read or accept unsolicited submissions
of ideas, stories, or artwork. For information regarding the
CPSIA on this printed material, call: (203) 595-3636 and
provide reference #RICH – 875962.

BOOM! Studios, 5670 Wilshire Boulevard, Suite 450, Los
Angeles, CA 90036-5679. Printed in USA. First Printing.

ISBN: 978-1-68415-496-8
eISBN: 978-1-64144-654-9

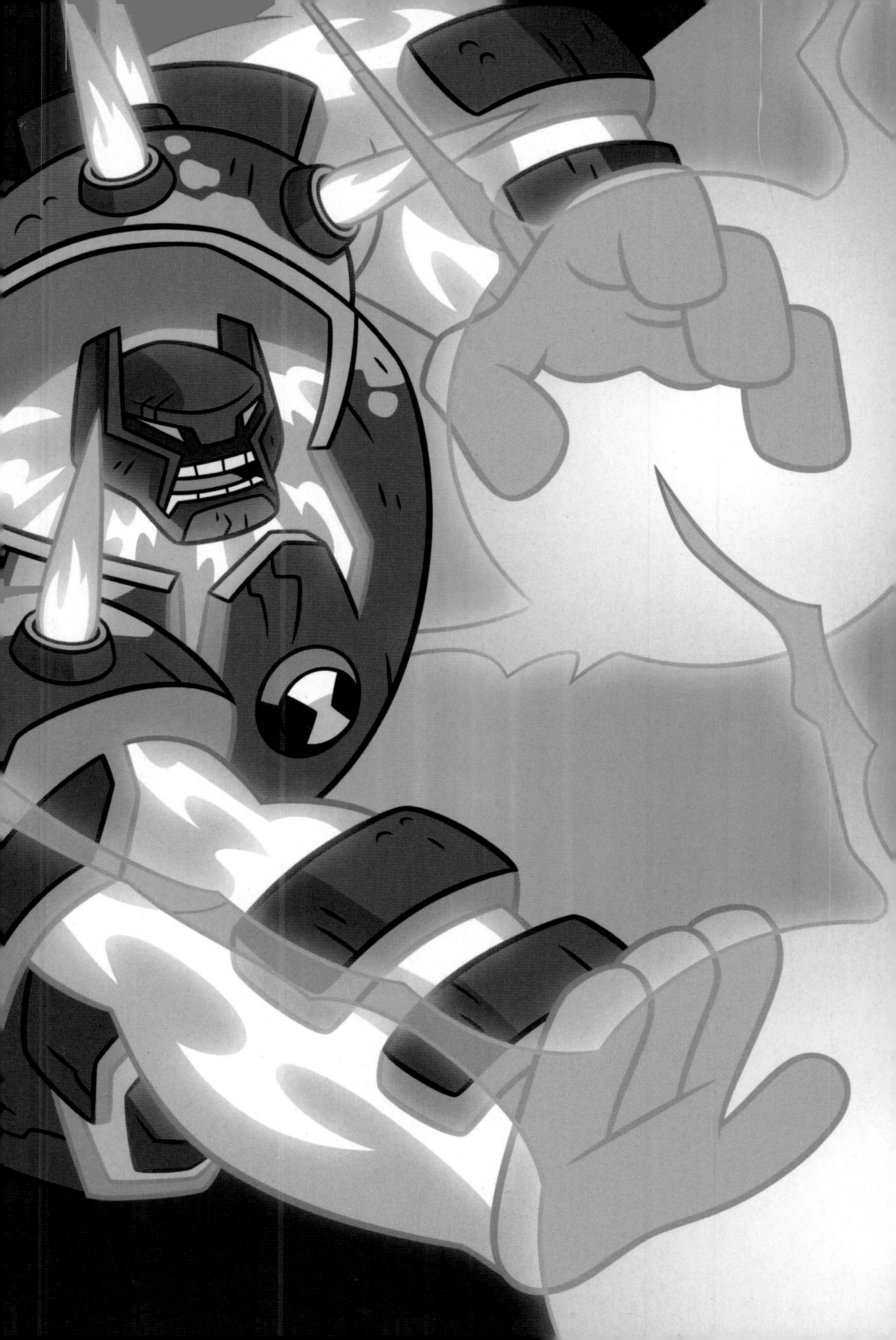

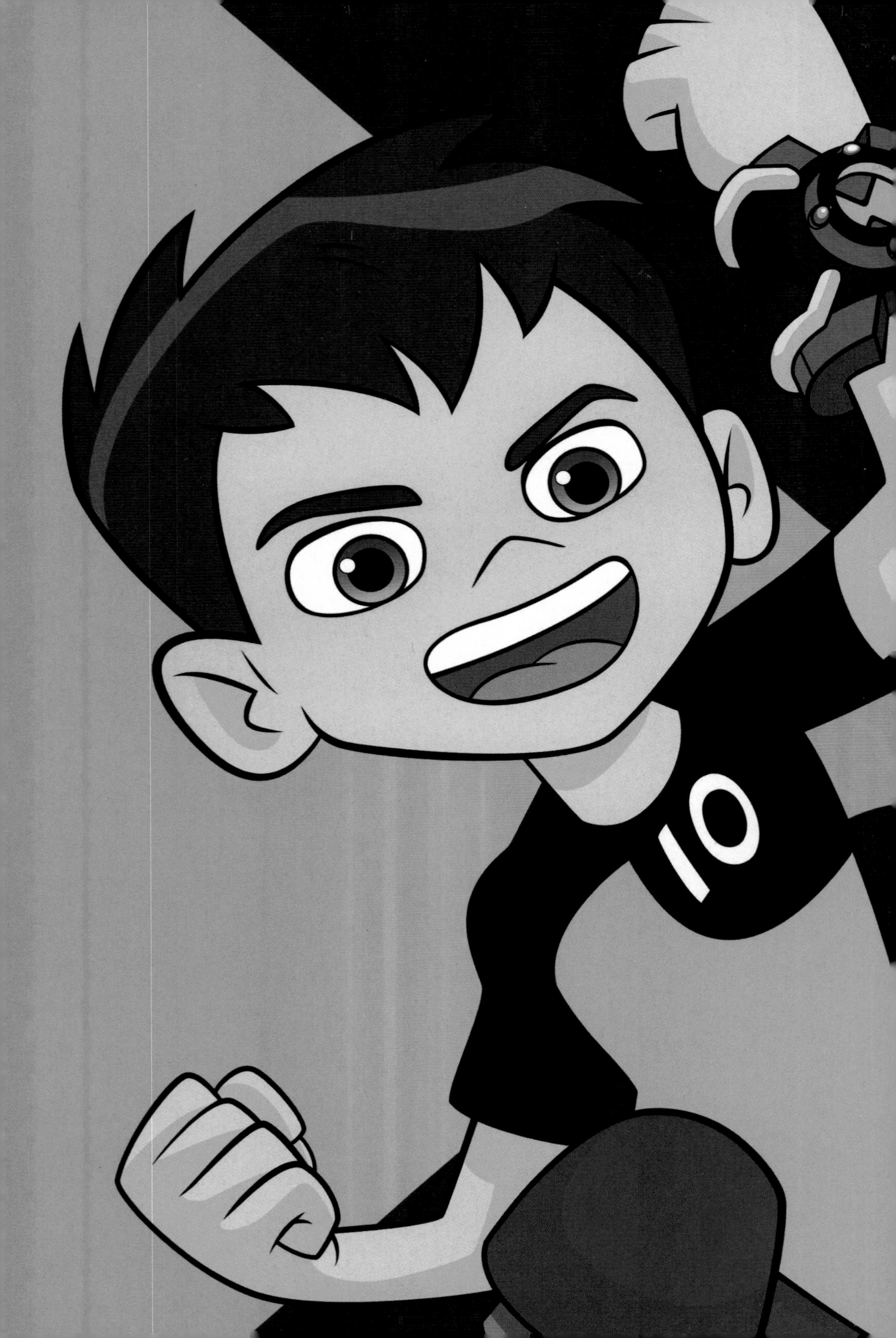
10

BEN TENNYSON IN...

THE MANCHESTER MYSTERY

CREATED BY
MAN OF ACTION

WRITTEN BY
C.B. LEE

ILLUSTRATED BY
FRANCESCA PERRONE

COLORED BY
ELEONORA BRUNI

LETTERED BY
WARREN MONTGOMERY

COVER BY
MATTIA DI MEO

DESIGNER
JILLIAN CRAB

EDITOR
MATTHEW LEVINE

WITH SPECIAL THANKS TO
MARISA MARIONAKIS, JANET NO,
AUSTIN PAGE, TRAMM WIGZELL,
KEITH FAY, SHAREENA CARLSON,
AND THE WONDERFUL FOLKS AT
CARTOON NETWORK.

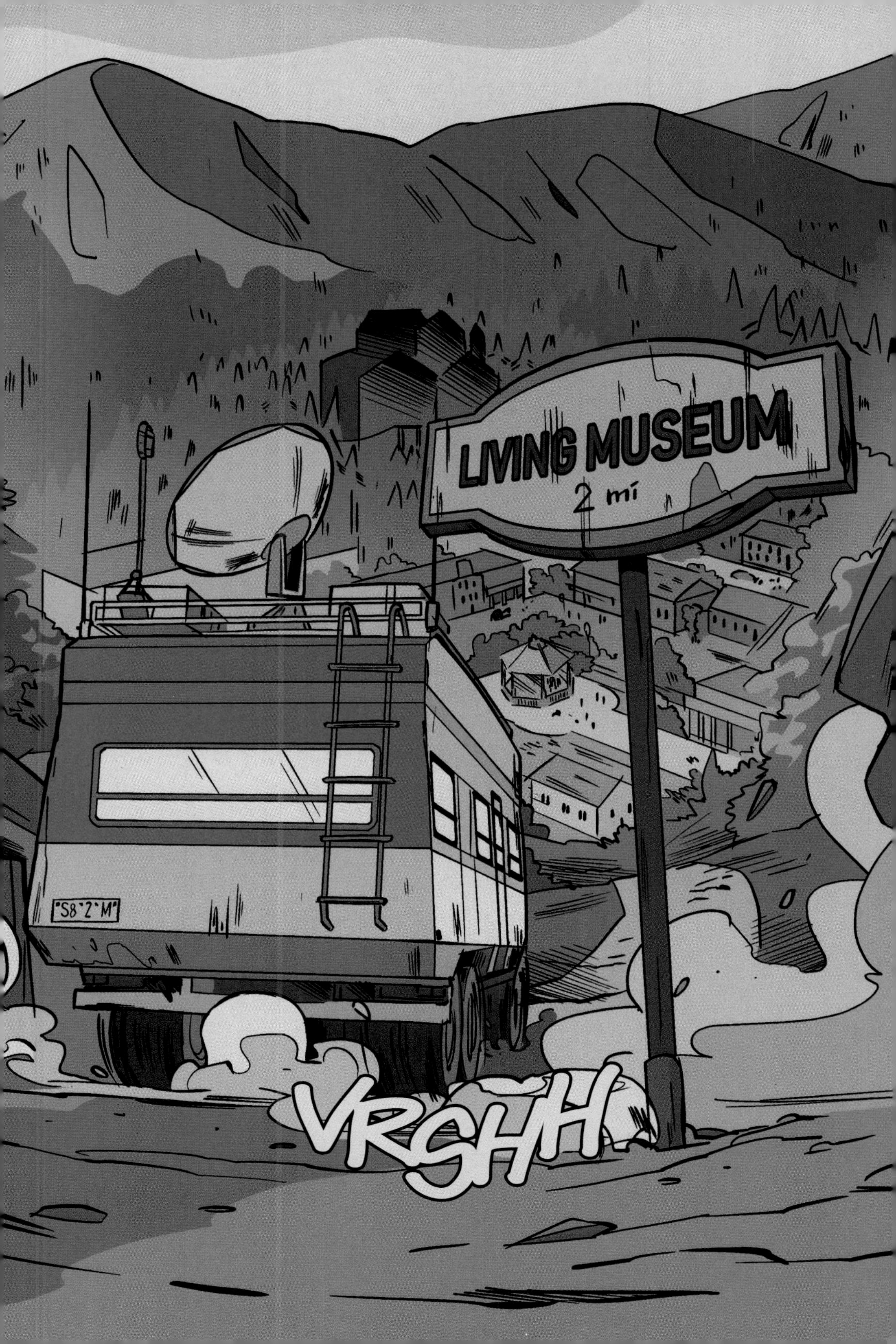
LIVING MUSEUM
2 mi
VRSHH

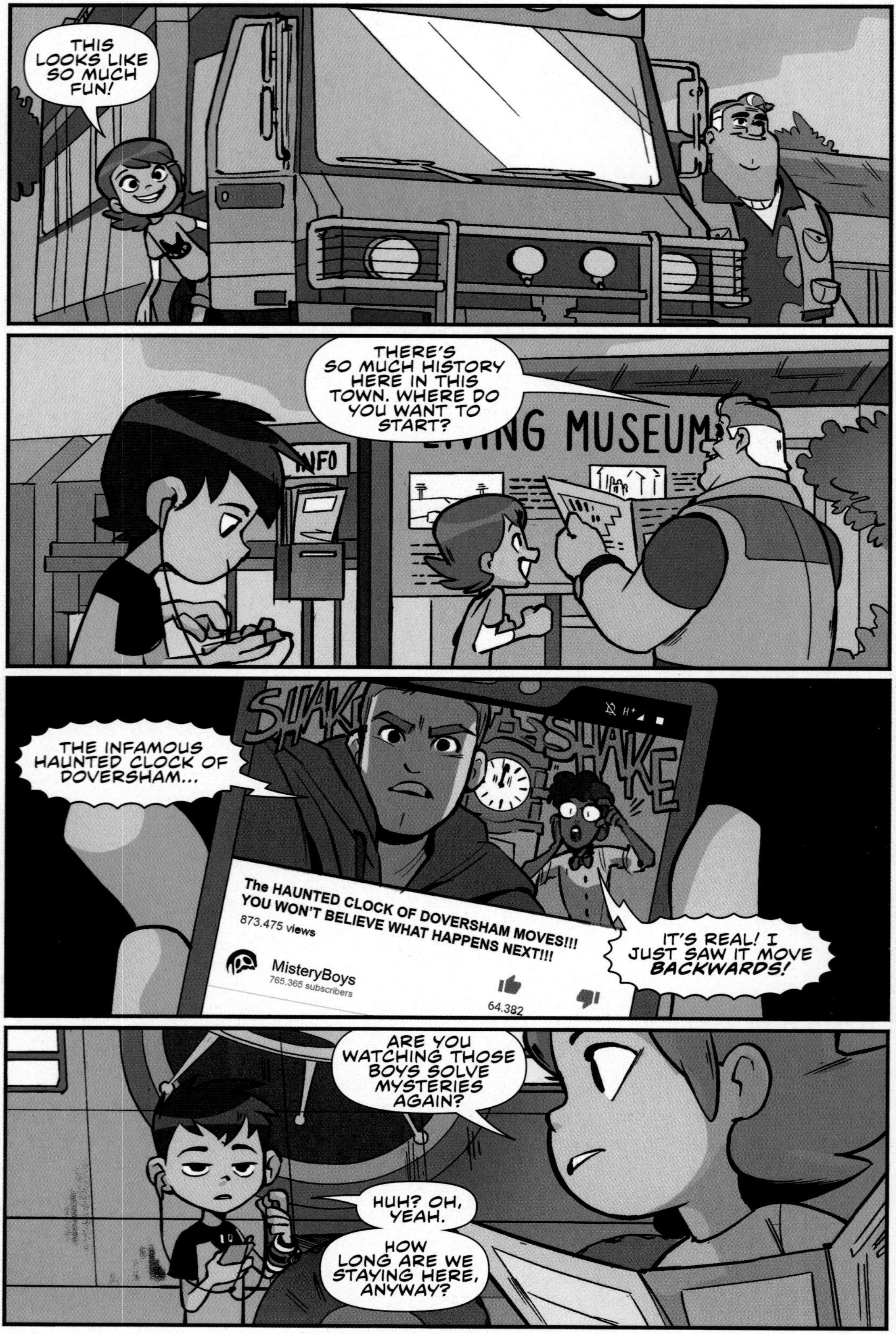
THIS LOOKS LIKE SO MUCH FUN!
THERE'S SO MUCH HISTORY HERE IN THIS TOWN. WHERE DO YOU WANT TO START?
LIVING MUSEUM
INFO
THE INFAMOUS HAUNTED CLOCK OF DOVERSHAM...
SHAKE SHAKE SHAKE
The HAUNTED CLOCK OF DOVERSHAM MOVES!!! YOU WON'T BELIEVE WHAT HAPPENS NEXT!!!
873.475 views
MisteryBoys
765.365 subscribers
64.382
IT'S REAL! I JUST SAW IT MOVE BACKWARDS!
ARE YOU WATCHING THOSE BOYS SOLVE MYSTERIES AGAIN?
HUH? OH, YEAH.
HOW LONG ARE WE STAYING HERE, ANYWAY?

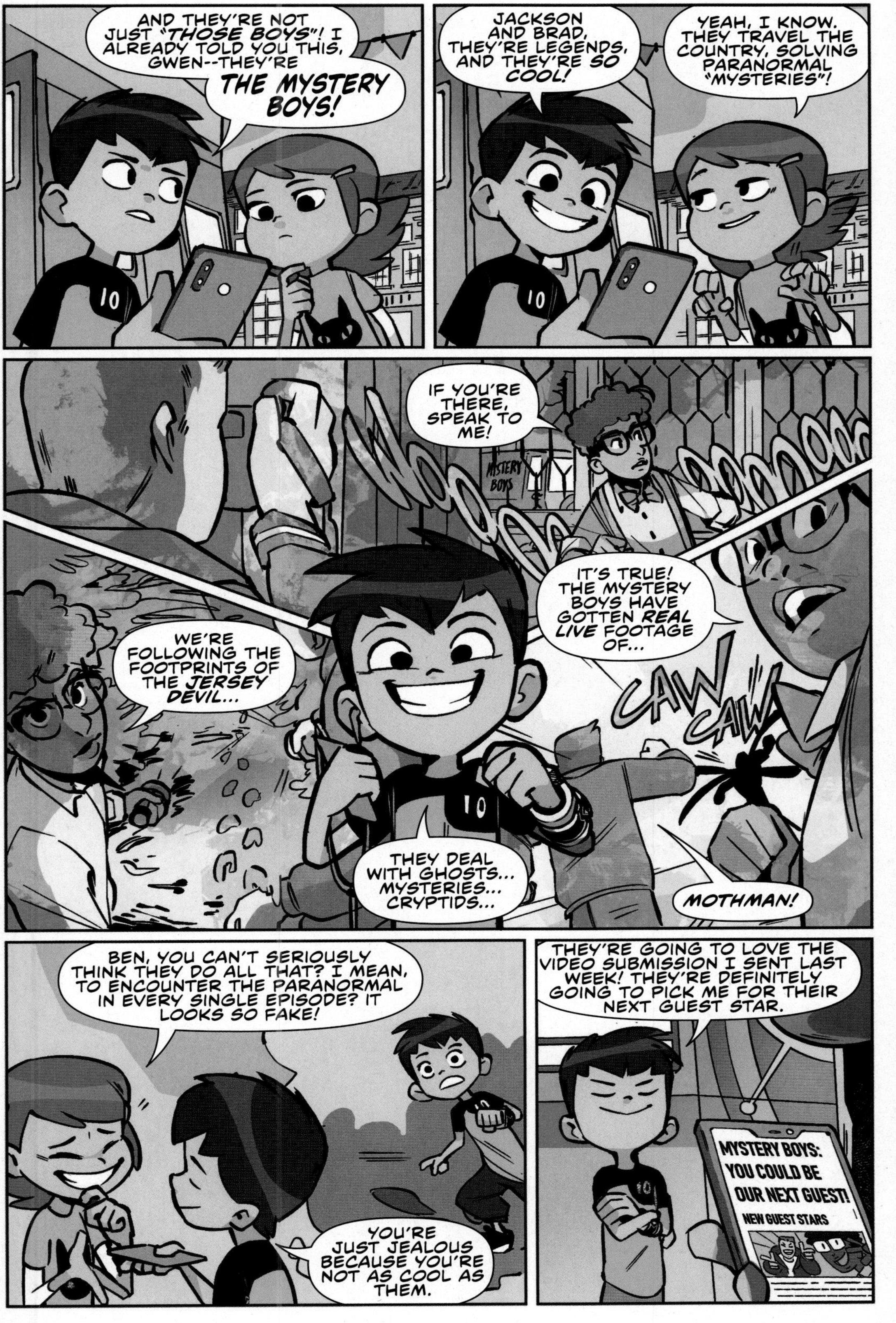
AND THEY'RE NOT JUST "THOSE BOYS"! I ALREADY TOLD YOU THIS, GWEN--THEY'RE THE MYSTERY BOYS!
JACKSON AND BRAD, THEY'RE LEGENDS, AND THEY'RE SO COOL!
YEAH, I KNOW. THEY TRAVEL THE COUNTRY, SOLVING PARANORMAL "MYSTERIES"!
IF YOU'RE THERE, SPEAK TO ME!
MYSTERY BOYS
WOOOOOOOOOOOOOOOOOOO
WE'RE FOLLOWING THE FOOTPRINTS OF THE JERSEY DEVIL...
IT'S TRUE! THE MYSTERY BOYS HAVE GOTTEN REAL LIVE FOOTAGE OF...
CAW CAW
THEY DEAL WITH GHOSTS... MYSTERIES... CRYPTIDS...
MOTHMAN!
BEN, YOU CAN'T SERIOUSLY THINK THEY DO ALL THAT? I MEAN, TO ENCOUNTER THE PARANORMAL IN EVERY SINGLE EPISODE? IT LOOKS SO FAKE!
YOU'RE JUST JEALOUS BECAUSE YOU'RE NOT AS COOL AS THEM.
THEY'RE GOING TO LOVE THE VIDEO SUBMISSION I SENT LAST WEEK! THEY'RE DEFINITELY GOING TO PICK ME FOR THEIR NEXT GUEST STAR.
MYSTERY BOYS: YOU COULD BE OUR NEXT GUEST!
NEW GUEST STARS

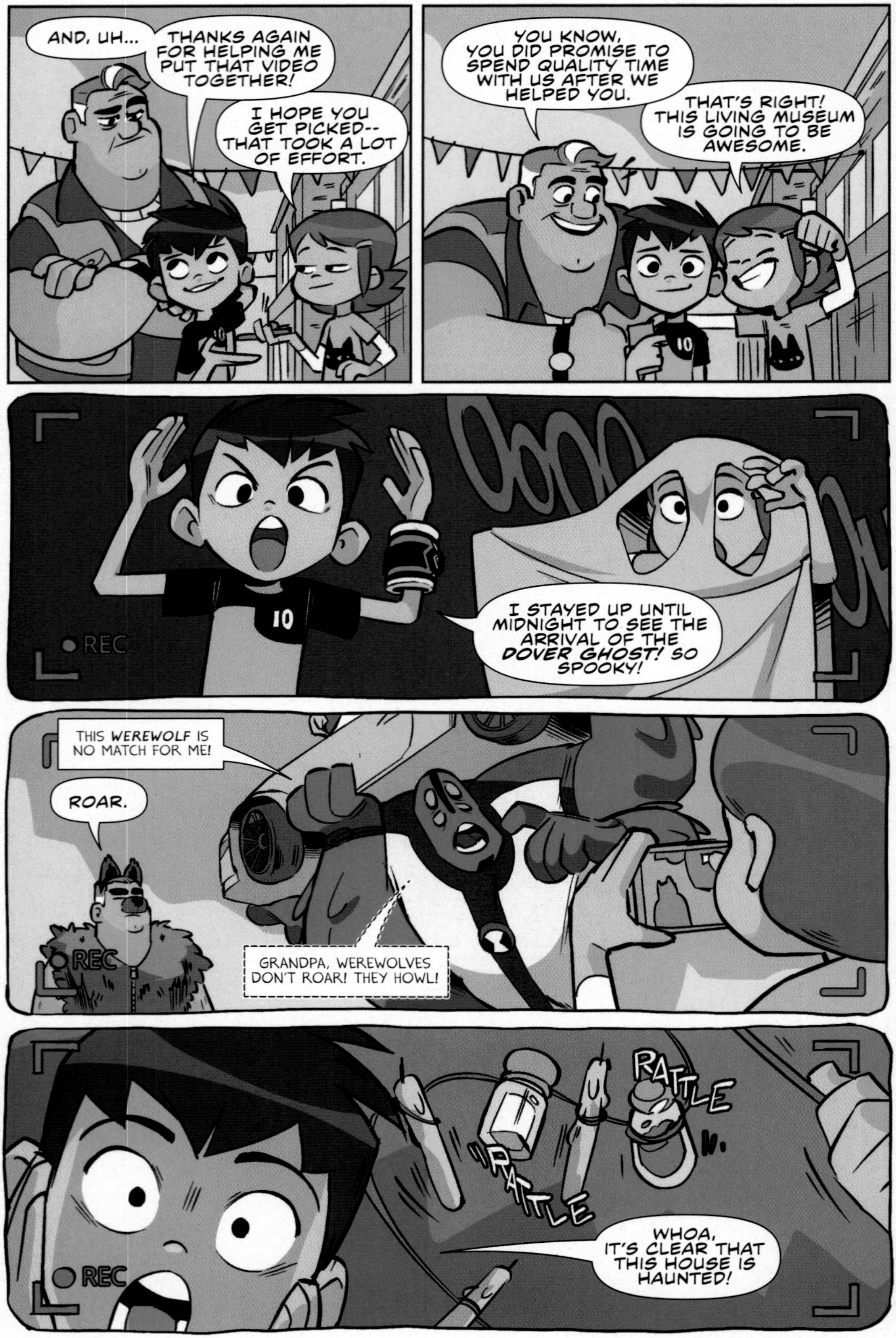

AND, UH...
THANKS AGAIN FOR HELPING ME PUT THAT VIDEO TOGETHER!
I HOPE YOU GET PICKED-- THAT TOOK A LOT OF EFFORT.
YOU KNOW, YOU DID PROMISE TO SPEND QUALITY TIME WITH US AFTER WE HELPED YOU.
THAT'S RIGHT! THIS LIVING MUSEUM IS GOING TO BE AWESOME.
REC
I STAYED UP UNTIL MIDNIGHT TO SEE THE ARRIVAL OF THE DOVER GHOST! SO SPOOKY!
THIS WEREWOLF IS NO MATCH FOR ME!
ROAR.
REC
GRANDPA, WEREWOLVES DON'T ROAR! THEY HOWL!
RATTLE
RATTLE
REC
WHOA, IT'S CLEAR THAT THIS HOUSE IS HAUNTED!

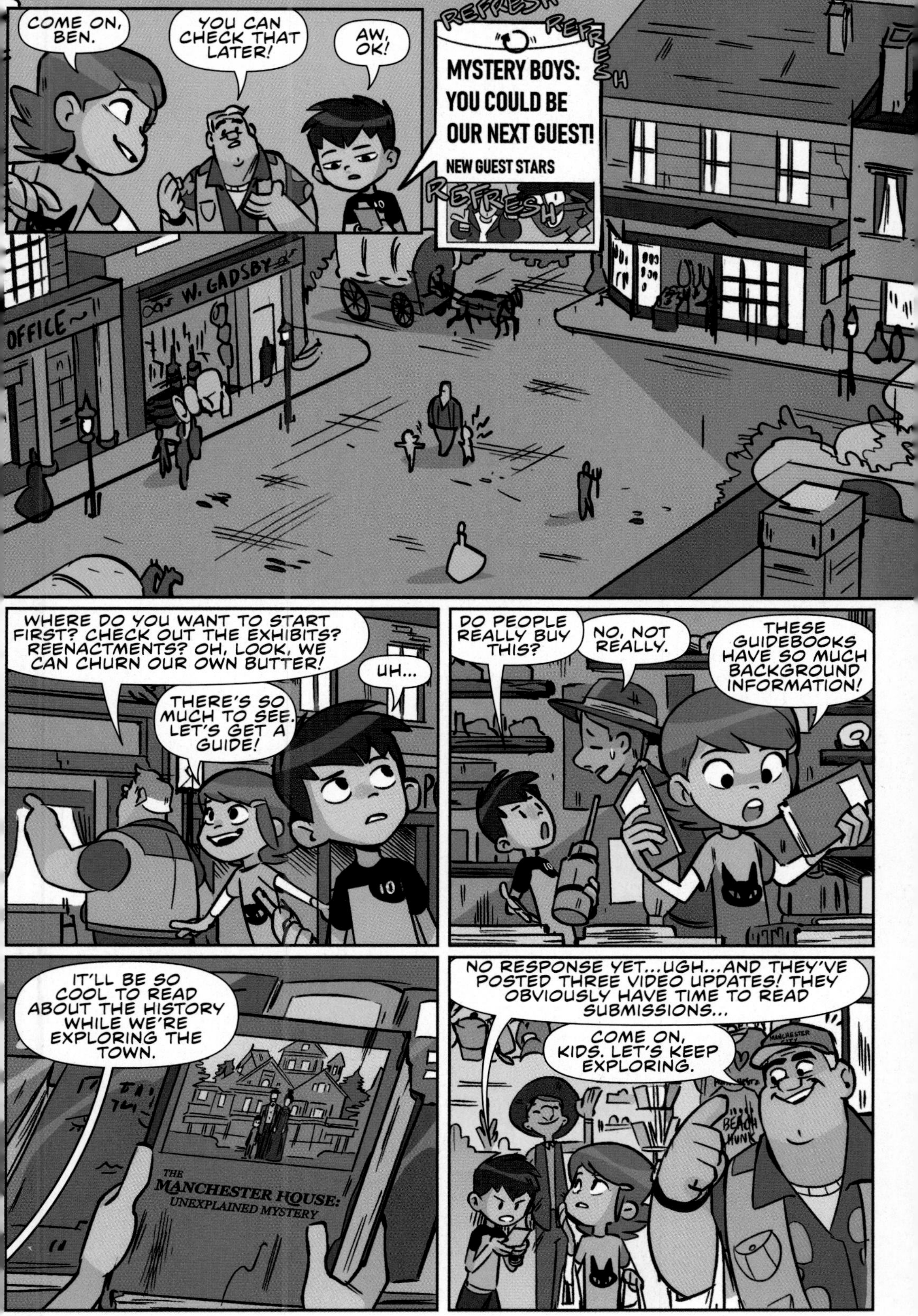

COME ON, BEN.
YOU CAN CHECK THAT LATER!
AW, OK!
REFRESH REFRESH
MYSTERY BOYS: YOU COULD BE OUR NEXT GUEST!
NEW GUEST STARS
REFRESH
W. GADSBY
OFFICE
WHERE DO YOU WANT TO START FIRST? CHECK OUT THE EXHIBITS? REENACTMENTS? OH, LOOK, WE CAN CHURN OUR OWN BUTTER!
UH...
THERE'S SO MUCH TO SEE. LET'S GET A GUIDE!
DO PEOPLE REALLY BUY THIS?
NO, NOT REALLY.
THESE GUIDEBOOKS HAVE SO MUCH BACKGROUND INFORMATION!
IT'LL BE SO COOL TO READ ABOUT THE HISTORY WHILE WE'RE EXPLORING THE TOWN.
THE MANCHESTER HOUSE: UNEXPLAINED MYSTERY
NO RESPONSE YET...UGH...AND THEY'VE POSTED THREE VIDEO UPDATES! THEY OBVIOUSLY HAVE TIME TO READ SUBMISSIONS...
COME ON, KIDS. LET'S KEEP EXPLORING.
MANCHESTER CITY
BEACH HUNK

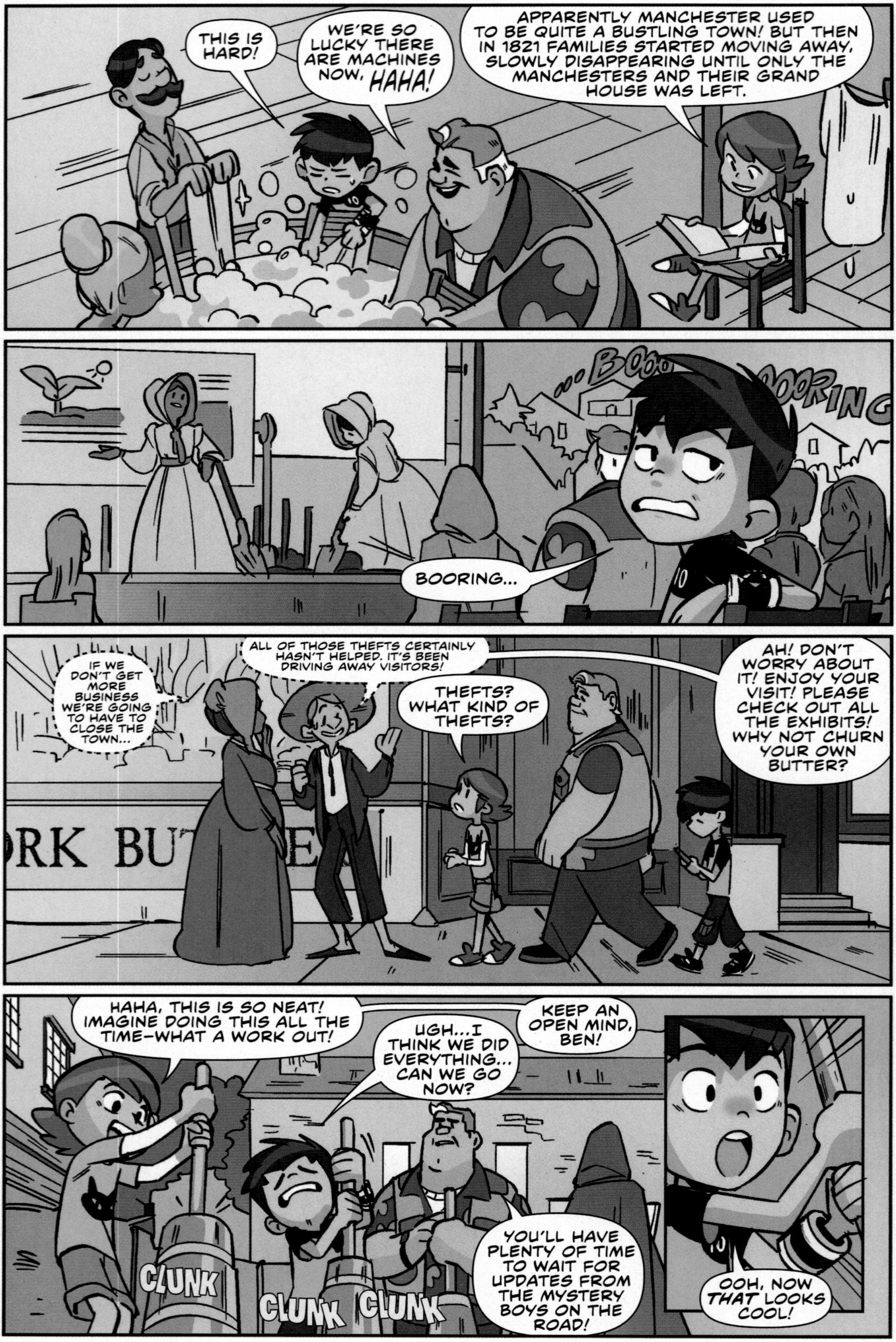
THIS IS HARD!
WE'RE SO LUCKY THERE ARE MACHINES NOW. HAHA!
APPARENTLY MANCHESTER USED TO BE QUITE A BUSTLING TOWN! BUT THEN IN 1821 FAMILIES STARTED MOVING AWAY, SLOWLY DISAPPEARING UNTIL ONLY THE MANCHESTERS AND THEIR GRAND HOUSE WAS LEFT.
BOOORING
BOORING...
IF WE DON'T GET MORE BUSINESS WE'RE GOING TO HAVE TO CLOSE THE TOWN...
ALL OF THOSE THEFTS CERTAINLY HASN'T HELPED. IT'S BEEN DRIVING AWAY VISITORS!
THEFTS? WHAT KIND OF THEFTS?
AH! DON'T WORRY ABOUT IT! ENJOY YOUR VISIT! PLEASE CHECK OUT ALL THE EXHIBITS! WHY NOT CHURN YOUR OWN BUTTER?
HAHA, THIS IS SO NEAT! IMAGINE DOING THIS ALL THE TIME—WHAT A WORK OUT!
KEEP AN OPEN MIND, BEN!
UGH...I THINK WE DID EVERYTHING... CAN WE GO NOW?
CLUNK
CLUNK CLUNK
YOU'LL HAVE PLENTY OF TIME TO WAIT FOR UPDATES FROM THE MYSTERY BOYS ON THE ROAD!
OOH, NOW THAT LOOKS COOL!

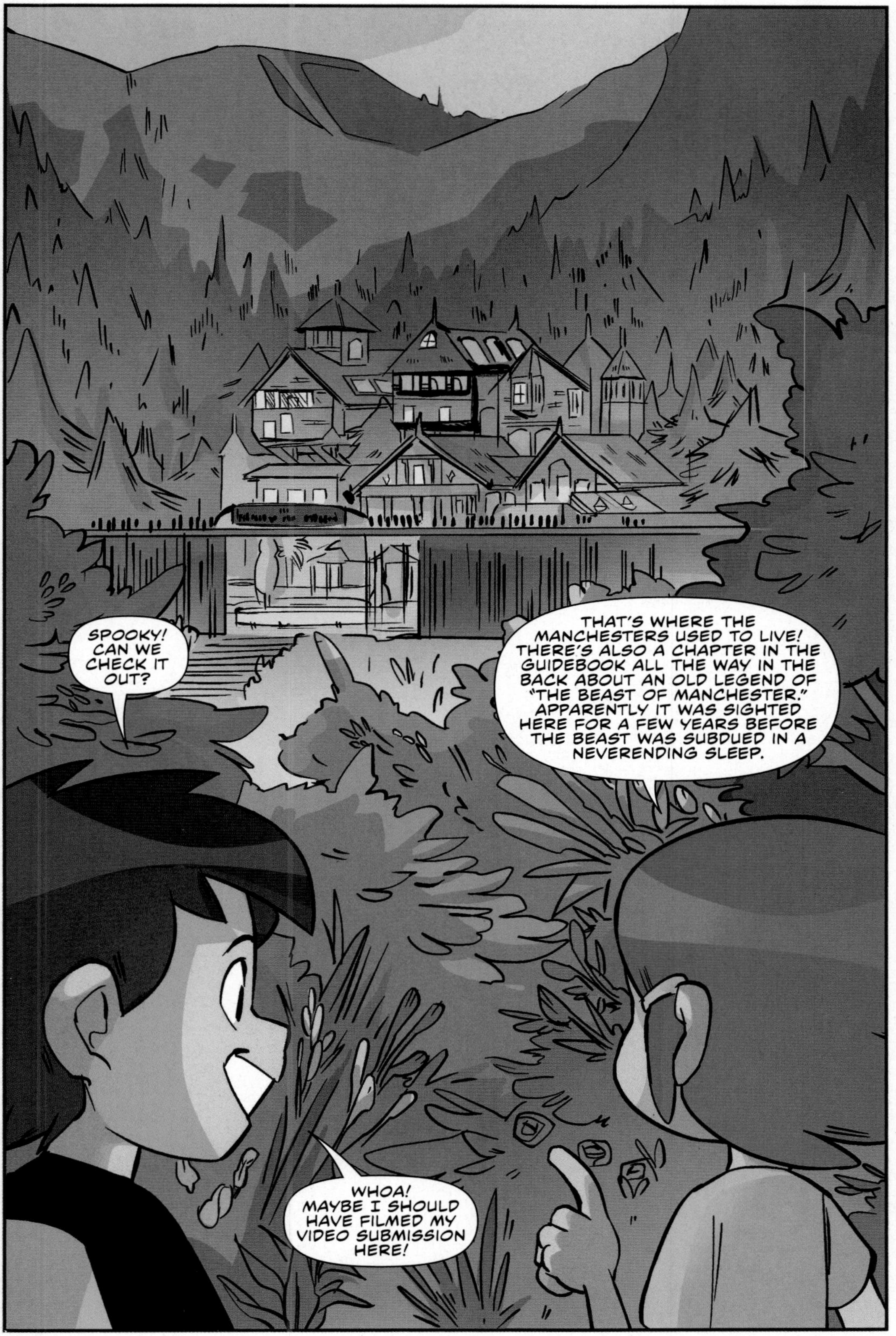
SPOOKY! CAN WE CHECK IT OUT?
THAT'S WHERE THE MANCHESTERS USED TO LIVE! THERE'S ALSO A CHAPTER IN THE GUIDEBOOK ALL THE WAY IN THE BACK ABOUT AN OLD LEGEND OF "THE BEAST OF MANCHESTER." APPARENTLY IT WAS SIGHTED HERE FOR A FEW YEARS BEFORE THE BEAST WAS SUBDUED IN A NEVERENDING SLEEP.
WHOA! MAYBE I SHOULD HAVE FILMED MY VIDEO SUBMISSION HERE!

THEY SHOULD PUT THAT BEAST THING IN THE TOUR GUIDE!

I DON'T KNOW. THIS CHAPTER ON IT IS PRETTY INTENSE.

A LOT MORE PEOPLE WOULD COME CHECK OUT A HAUNTED TOWN.

THE MANCHESTER HOUSE

THE RESIDENTS WERE TERRIFIED BY A SHADOWY WOLF CREATURE THAT SEEMED TO DISAPPEAR DURING THE DAY LIKE A GHOST.

GUIDED TOURS
DAYTIME
AND
NIG

THE BEAST OF MANCHESTER WAS OFTEN SEEN LURKING AROUND THE GROUNDS. THE MANCHESTER FAMILY WAS FEARED BECAUSE OF THE SIGHTINGS. IT WAS RUMORED THEY COULD EVEN COULD CONTROL IT...

SO IT ONLY CAME OUT AT NIGHT, HUH! WAIT, DID YOU SAY IT WAS IN NEVER-ENDING SLEEP?

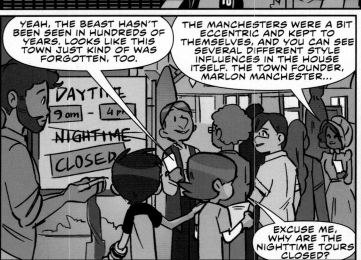

YEAH, THE BEAST HASN'T BEEN SEEN IN HUNDREDS OF YEARS. LOOKS LIKE THIS TOWN JUST KIND OF WAS FORGOTTEN, TOO.

THE MANCHESTERS WERE A BIT ECCENTRIC AND KEPT TO THEMSELVES, AND YOU CAN SEE SEVERAL DIFFERENT STYLE INFLUENCES IN THE HOUSE ITSELF. THE TOWN FOUNDER, MARLON MANCHESTER...

DAYTIME
9 am - 4 p
NIGHTTIME
CLOSED

EXCUSE ME, WHY ARE THE NIGHTTIME TOURS CLOSED?

WELL, A FEW...UNEXPLAINABLE INCIDENTS. MANY ITEMS HAVE JUST VANISHED IN THE MIDDLE OF THE NIGHT.

NONE OF THE EMPLOYEES WANT TO WORK THE NIGHT SHIFT.

HOW MYSTERIOUS! MAYBE IT'S A...GHOSTLY *BEAST!*

IT'S A DEFINITELY A GHOST, I TELL YA! THE MIRRORS HAVE GONE MISSING, ALL THE VASES AND CUPS...I FEEL THE COLD SPOTS TOO.

IT'S GOING TO BE DARK IN A FEW HOURS...I THINK WE SHOULD STAY TO CHECK IT OUT!

THE THEFTS? YEAH, IT SOUNDS LIKE A GOOD CASE.

I THINK IT'S THE WORK OF SOMETHING PARANORMAL--LIKE THE BEAST OF MANCHESTER!

HMM MAYBE, BUT IT'S WORTH TAKING A LOOK!

WHAT WAS THAT!?

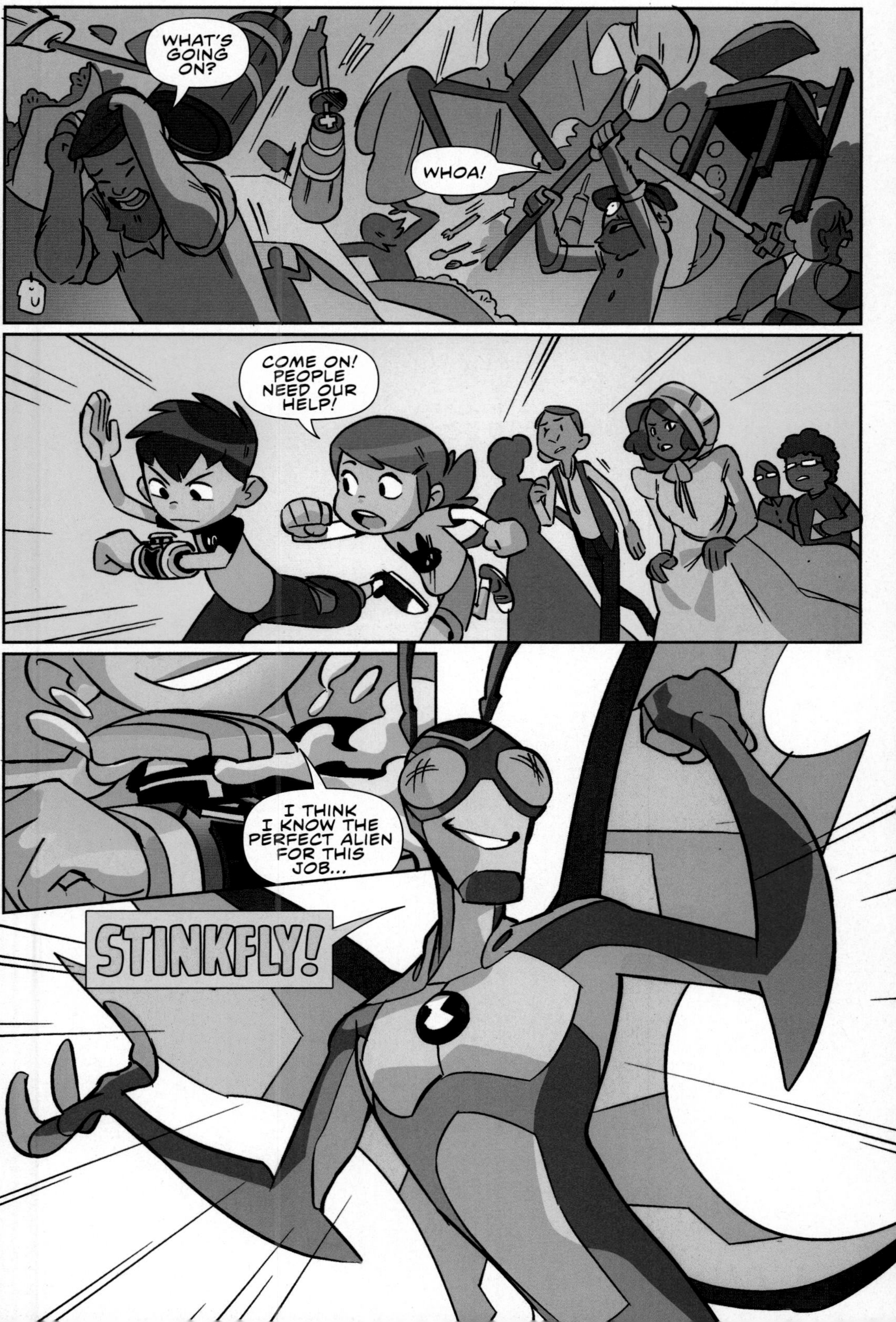
WHAT'S GOING ON?
WHOA!
COME ON! PEOPLE NEED OUR HELP!
I THINK I KNOW THE PERFECT ALIEN FOR THIS JOB...
STINKFLY!

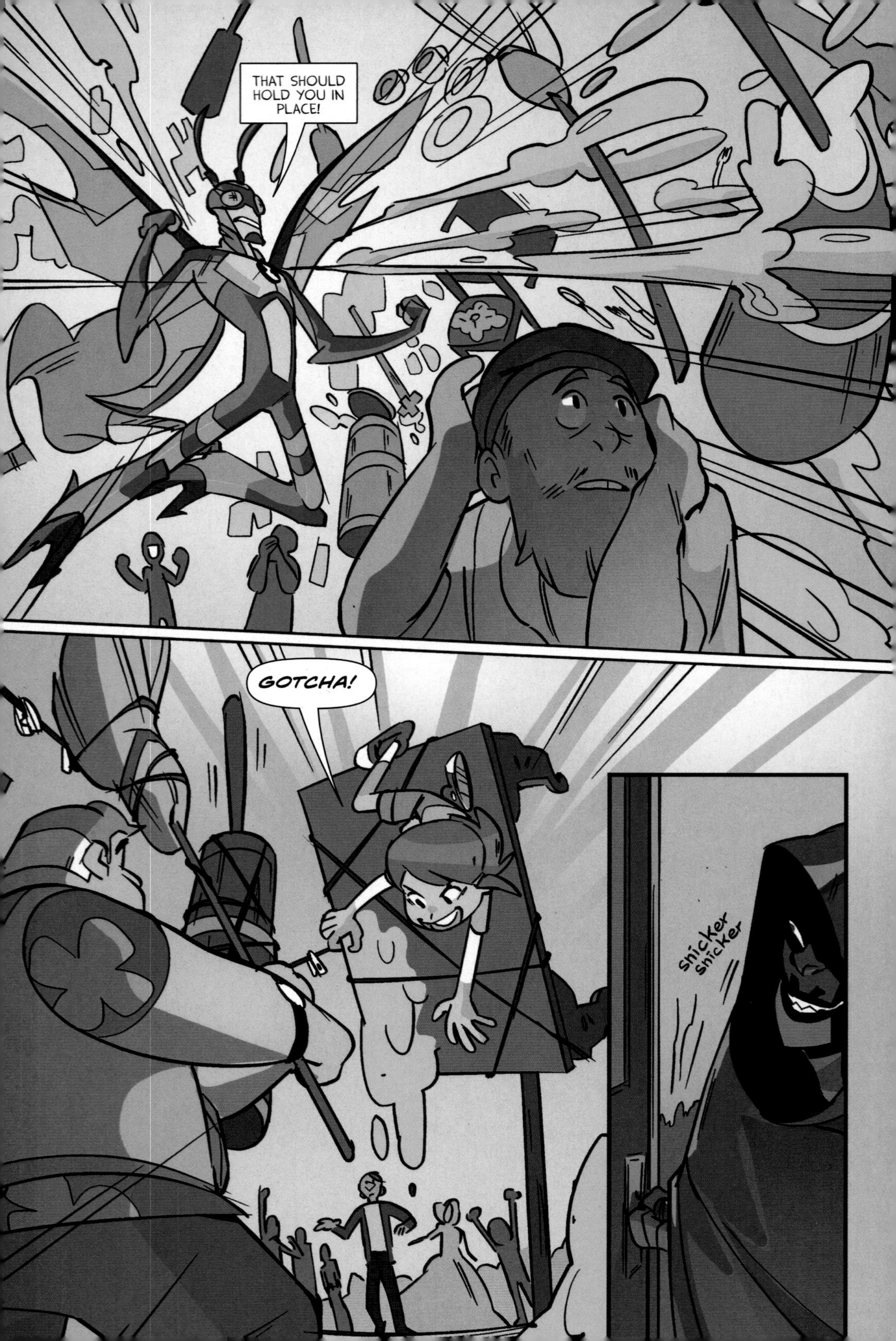
THAT SHOULD HOLD YOU IN PLACE!
GOTCHA!
snicker snicker

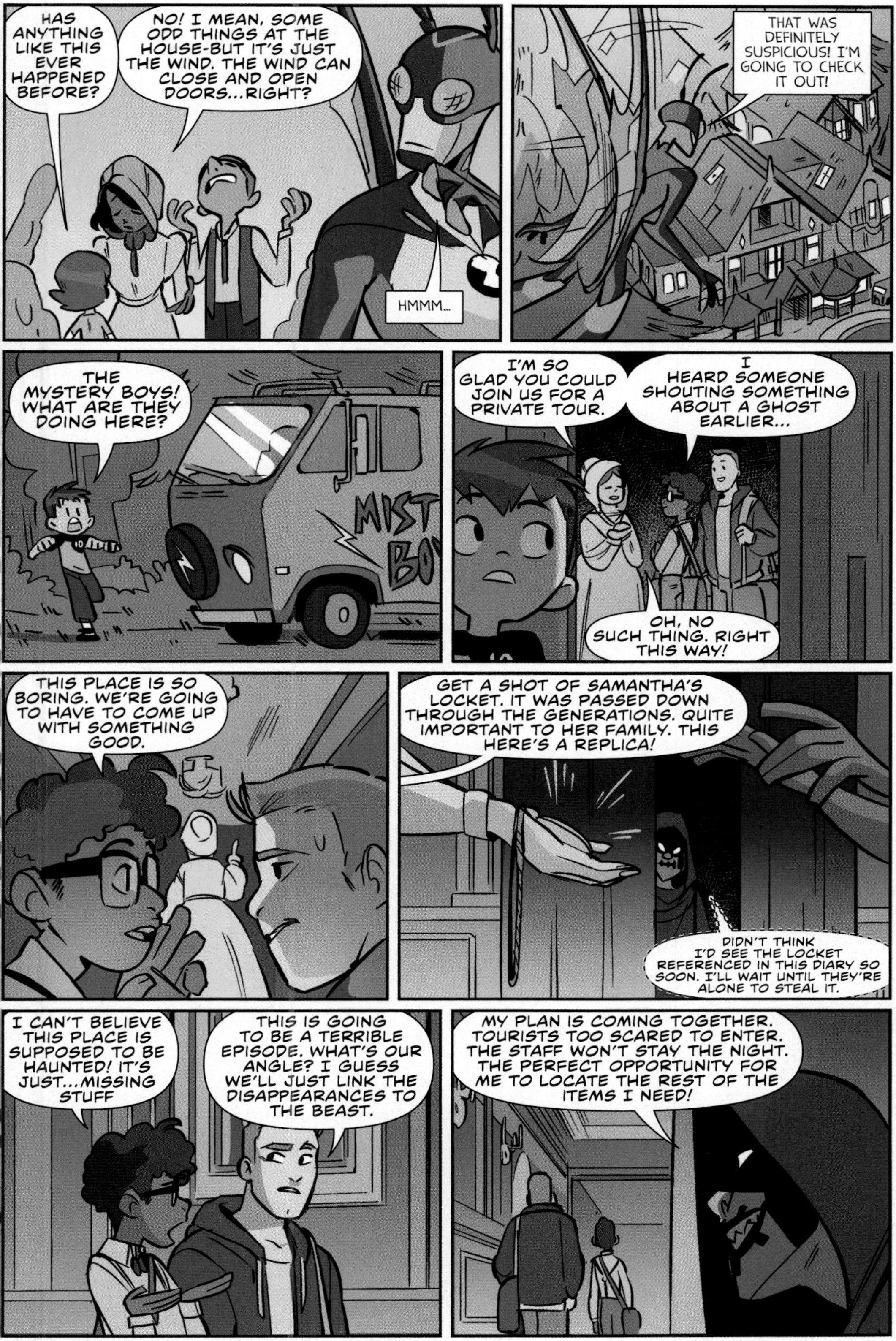
HAS ANYTHING LIKE THIS EVER HAPPENED BEFORE?
NO! I MEAN, SOME ODD THINGS AT THE HOUSE-BUT IT'S JUST THE WIND. THE WIND CAN CLOSE AND OPEN DOORS...RIGHT?
HMMM...
THAT WAS DEFINITELY SUSPICIOUS! I'M GOING TO CHECK IT OUT!
THE MYSTERY BOYS! WHAT ARE THEY DOING HERE?
MIST
BO
I'M SO GLAD YOU COULD JOIN US FOR A PRIVATE TOUR.
I HEARD SOMEONE SHOUTING SOMETHING ABOUT A GHOST EARLIER...
OH, NO SUCH THING. RIGHT THIS WAY!
THIS PLACE IS SO BORING. WE'RE GOING TO HAVE TO COME UP WITH SOMETHING GOOD.
GET A SHOT OF SAMANTHA'S LOCKET. IT WAS PASSED DOWN THROUGH THE GENERATIONS. QUITE IMPORTANT TO HER FAMILY. THIS HERE'S A REPLICA!
DIDN'T THINK I'D SEE THE LOCKET REFERENCED IN THIS DIARY SO SOON. I'LL WAIT UNTIL THEY'RE ALONE TO STEAL IT.
I CAN'T BELIEVE THIS PLACE IS SUPPOSED TO BE HAUNTED! IT'S JUST...MISSING STUFF
THIS IS GOING TO BE A TERRIBLE EPISODE. WHAT'S OUR ANGLE? I GUESS WE'LL JUST LINK THE DISAPPEARANCES TO THE BEAST.
MY PLAN IS COMING TOGETHER. TOURISTS TOO SCARED TO ENTER. THE STAFF WON'T STAY THE NIGHT. THE PERFECT OPPORTUNITY FOR ME TO LOCATE THE REST OF THE ITEMS I NEED!

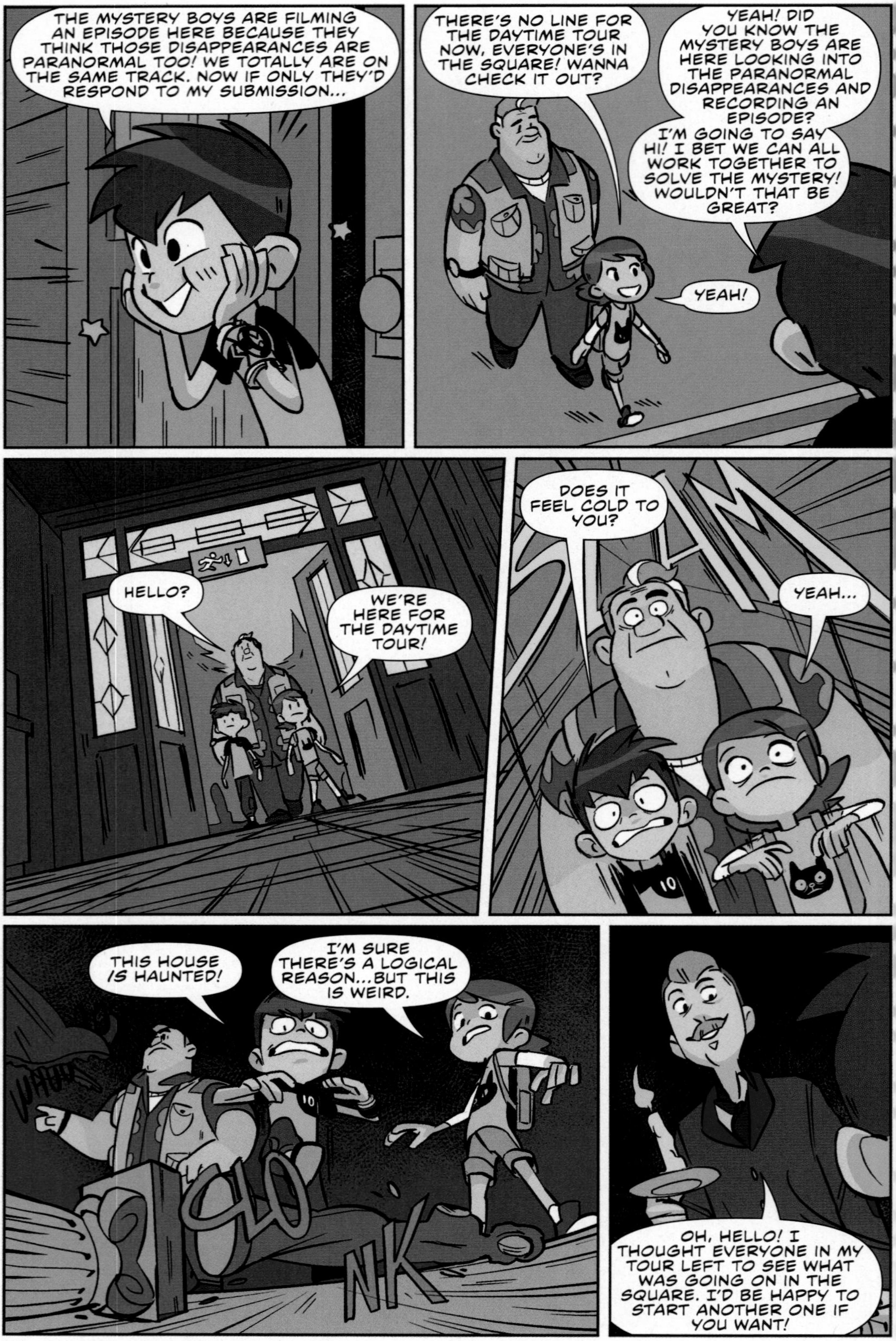
THE MYSTERY BOYS ARE FILMING AN EPISODE HERE BECAUSE THEY THINK THOSE DISAPPEARANCES ARE PARANORMAL TOO! WE TOTALLY ARE ON THE SAME TRACK. NOW IF ONLY THEY'D RESPOND TO MY SUBMISSION...
THERE'S NO LINE FOR THE DAYTIME TOUR NOW, EVERYONE'S IN THE SQUARE! WANNA CHECK IT OUT?
YEAH! DID YOU KNOW THE MYSTERY BOYS ARE HERE LOOKING INTO THE PARANORMAL DISAPPEARANCES AND RECORDING AN EPISODE?
I'M GOING TO SAY HI! I BET WE CAN ALL WORK TOGETHER TO SOLVE THE MYSTERY! WOULDN'T THAT BE GREAT?
YEAH!
HELLO?
WE'RE HERE FOR THE DAYTIME TOUR!
DOES IT FEEL COLD TO YOU?
YEAH...
THIS HOUSE IS HAUNTED!
I'M SURE THERE'S A LOGICAL REASON...BUT THIS IS WEIRD.
CLONK
OH, HELLO! I THOUGHT EVERYONE IN MY TOUR LEFT TO SEE WHAT WAS GOING ON IN THE SQUARE. I'D BE HAPPY TO START ANOTHER ONE IF YOU WANT!

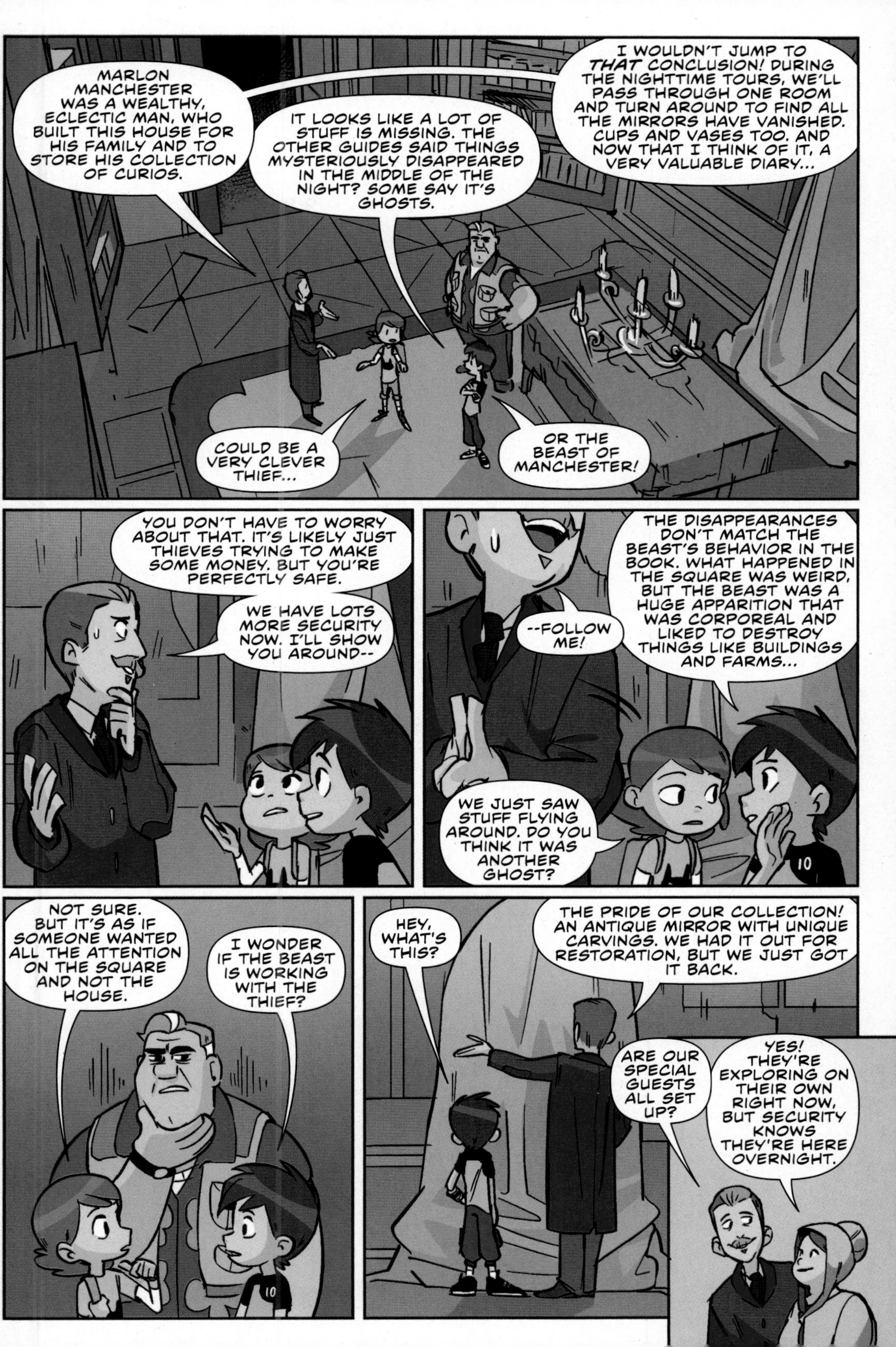
MARLON MANCHESTER WAS A WEALTHY, ECLECTIC MAN, WHO BUILT THIS HOUSE FOR HIS FAMILY AND TO STORE HIS COLLECTION OF CURIOS.
IT LOOKS LIKE A LOT OF STUFF IS MISSING. THE OTHER GUIDES SAID THINGS MYSTERIOUSLY DISAPPEARED IN THE MIDDLE OF THE NIGHT? SOME SAY IT'S GHOSTS.
I WOULDN'T JUMP TO *THAT* CONCLUSION! DURING THE NIGHTTIME TOURS, WE'LL PASS THROUGH ONE ROOM AND TURN AROUND TO FIND ALL THE MIRRORS HAVE VANISHED. CUPS AND VASES TOO. AND NOW THAT I THINK OF IT, A VERY VALUABLE DIARY...
COULD BE A VERY CLEVER THIEF...
OR THE BEAST OF MANCHESTER!
YOU DON'T HAVE TO WORRY ABOUT THAT. IT'S LIKELY JUST THIEVES TRYING TO MAKE SOME MONEY. BUT YOU'RE PERFECTLY SAFE.
WE HAVE LOTS MORE SECURITY NOW. I'LL SHOW YOU AROUND--
--FOLLOW ME!
THE DISAPPEARANCES DON'T MATCH THE BEAST'S BEHAVIOR IN THE BOOK. WHAT HAPPENED IN THE SQUARE WAS WEIRD, BUT THE BEAST WAS A HUGE APPARITION THAT WAS CORPOREAL AND LIKED TO DESTROY THINGS LIKE BUILDINGS AND FARMS...
WE JUST SAW STUFF FLYING AROUND. DO YOU THINK IT WAS ANOTHER GHOST?
10
NOT SURE. BUT IT'S AS IF SOMEONE WANTED ALL THE ATTENTION ON THE SQUARE AND NOT THE HOUSE.
I WONDER IF THE BEAST IS WORKING WITH THE THIEF?
10
HEY, WHAT'S THIS?
THE PRIDE OF OUR COLLECTION! AN ANTIQUE MIRROR WITH UNIQUE CARVINGS. WE HAD IT OUT FOR RESTORATION, BUT WE JUST GOT IT BACK.
ARE OUR SPECIAL GUESTS ALL SET UP?
YES! THEY'RE EXPLORING ON THEIR OWN RIGHT NOW, BUT SECURITY KNOWS THEY'RE HERE OVERNIGHT.

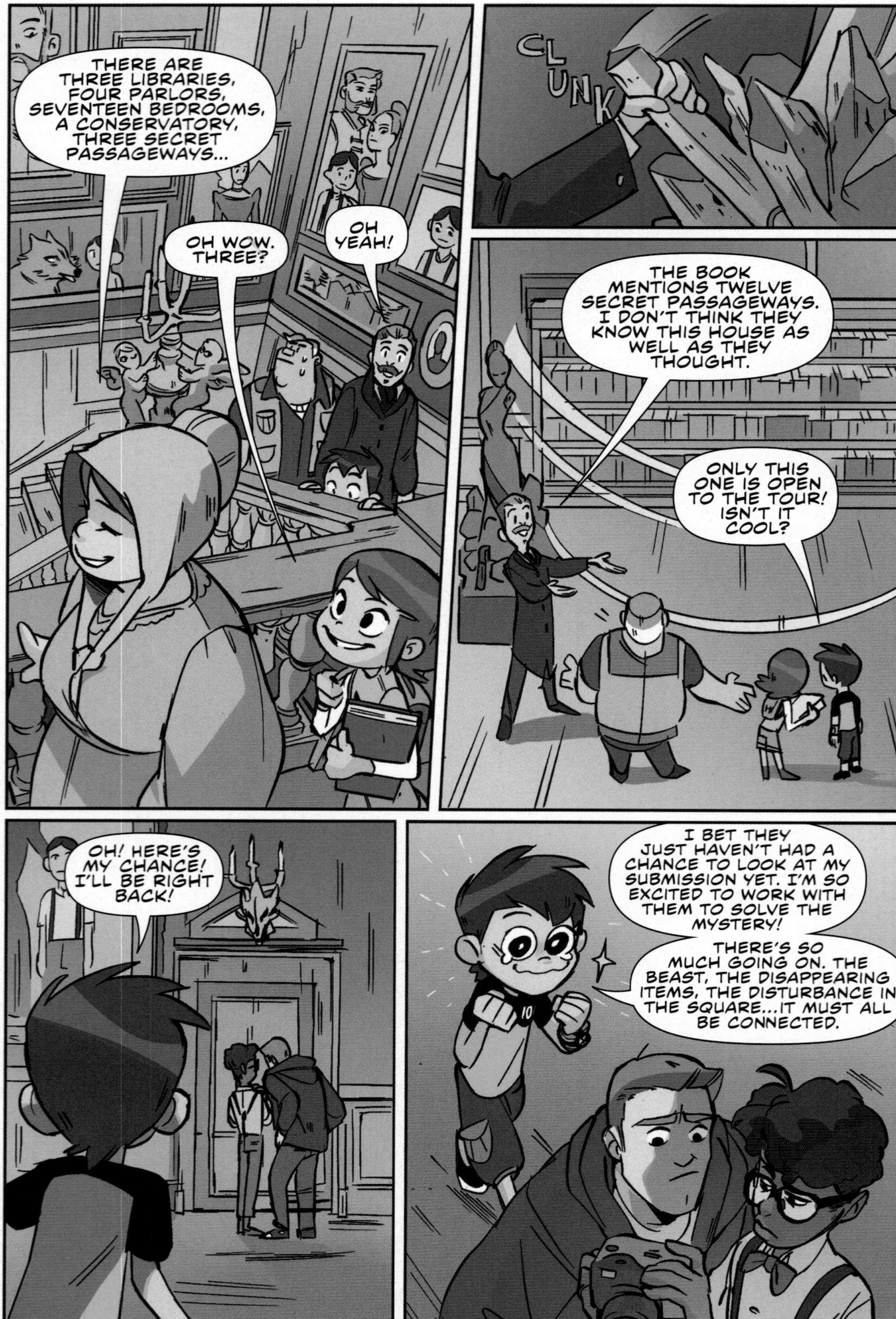
THERE ARE THREE LIBRARIES, FOUR PARLORS, SEVENTEEN BEDROOMS, A CONSERVATORY, THREE SECRET PASSAGEWAYS...
OH WOW. THREE?
OH YEAH!
CLUNK
THE BOOK MENTIONS TWELVE SECRET PASSAGEWAYS. I DON'T THINK THEY KNOW THIS HOUSE AS WELL AS THEY THOUGHT.
ONLY THIS ONE IS OPEN TO THE TOUR! ISN'T IT COOL?
OH! HERE'S MY CHANCE! I'LL BE RIGHT BACK!
I BET THEY JUST HAVEN'T HAD A CHANCE TO LOOK AT MY SUBMISSION YET. I'M SO EXCITED TO WORK WITH THEM TO SOLVE THE MYSTERY!
THERE'S SO MUCH GOING ON. THE BEAST, THE DISAPPEARING ITEMS, THE DISTURBANCE IN THE SQUARE...IT MUST ALL BE CONNECTED.

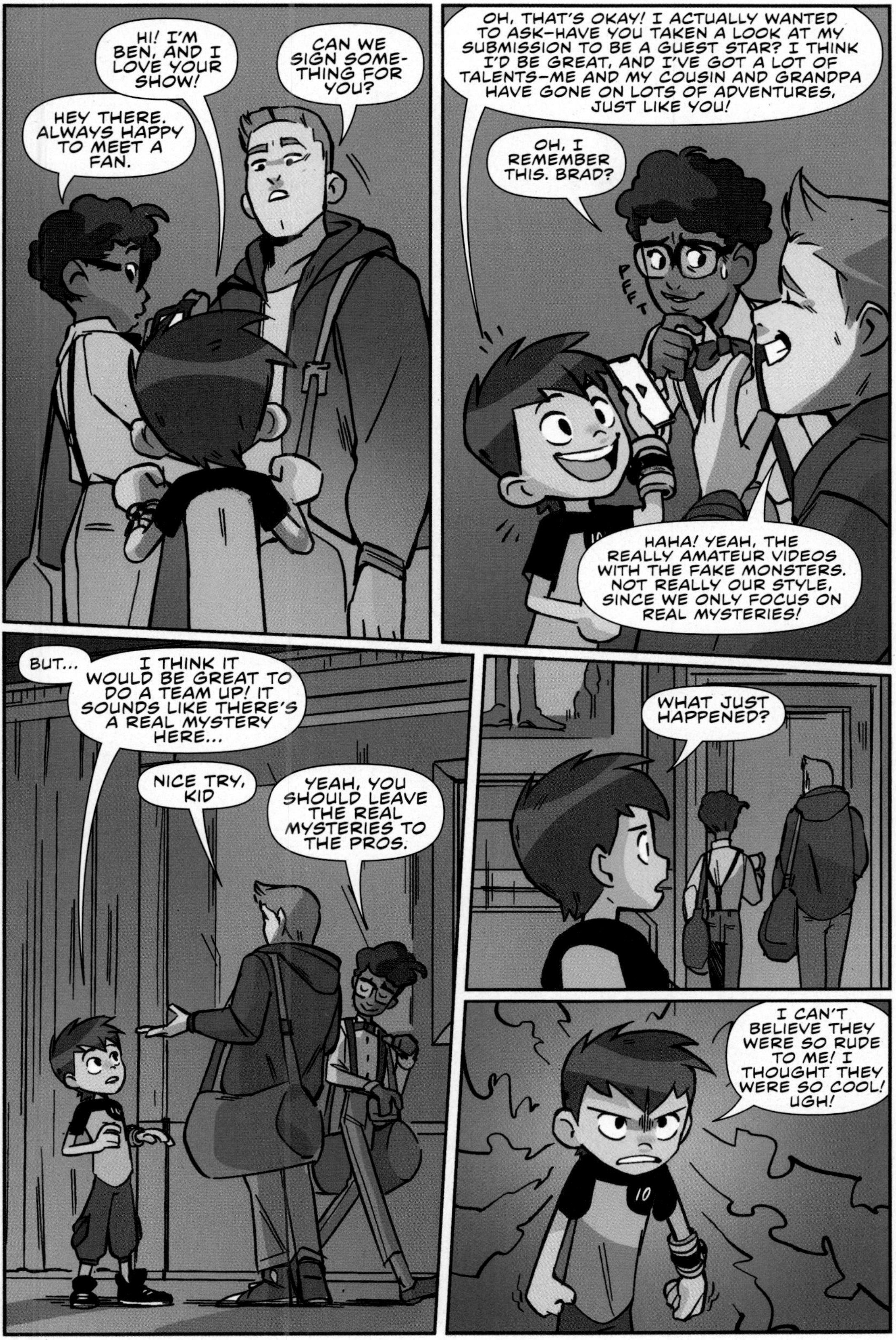
HI! I'M BEN, AND I LOVE YOUR SHOW!
CAN WE SIGN SOMETHING FOR YOU?
HEY THERE. ALWAYS HAPPY TO MEET A FAN.
OH, THAT'S OKAY! I ACTUALLY WANTED TO ASK–HAVE YOU TAKEN A LOOK AT MY SUBMISSION TO BE A GUEST STAR? I THINK I'D BE GREAT, AND I'VE GOT A LOT OF TALENTS–ME AND MY COUSIN AND GRANDPA HAVE GONE ON LOTS OF ADVENTURES, JUST LIKE YOU!
OH, I REMEMBER THIS. BRAD?
PFFT
HAHA! YEAH, THE REALLY AMATEUR VIDEOS WITH THE FAKE MONSTERS. NOT REALLY OUR STYLE, SINCE WE ONLY FOCUS ON REAL MYSTERIES!
BUT...
I THINK IT WOULD BE GREAT TO DO A TEAM UP! IT SOUNDS LIKE THERE'S A REAL MYSTERY HERE...
NICE TRY, KID
YEAH, YOU SHOULD LEAVE THE REAL MYSTERIES TO THE PROS.
WHAT JUST HAPPENED?
I CAN'T BELIEVE THEY WERE SO RUDE TO ME! I THOUGHT THEY WERE SO COOL! UGH!

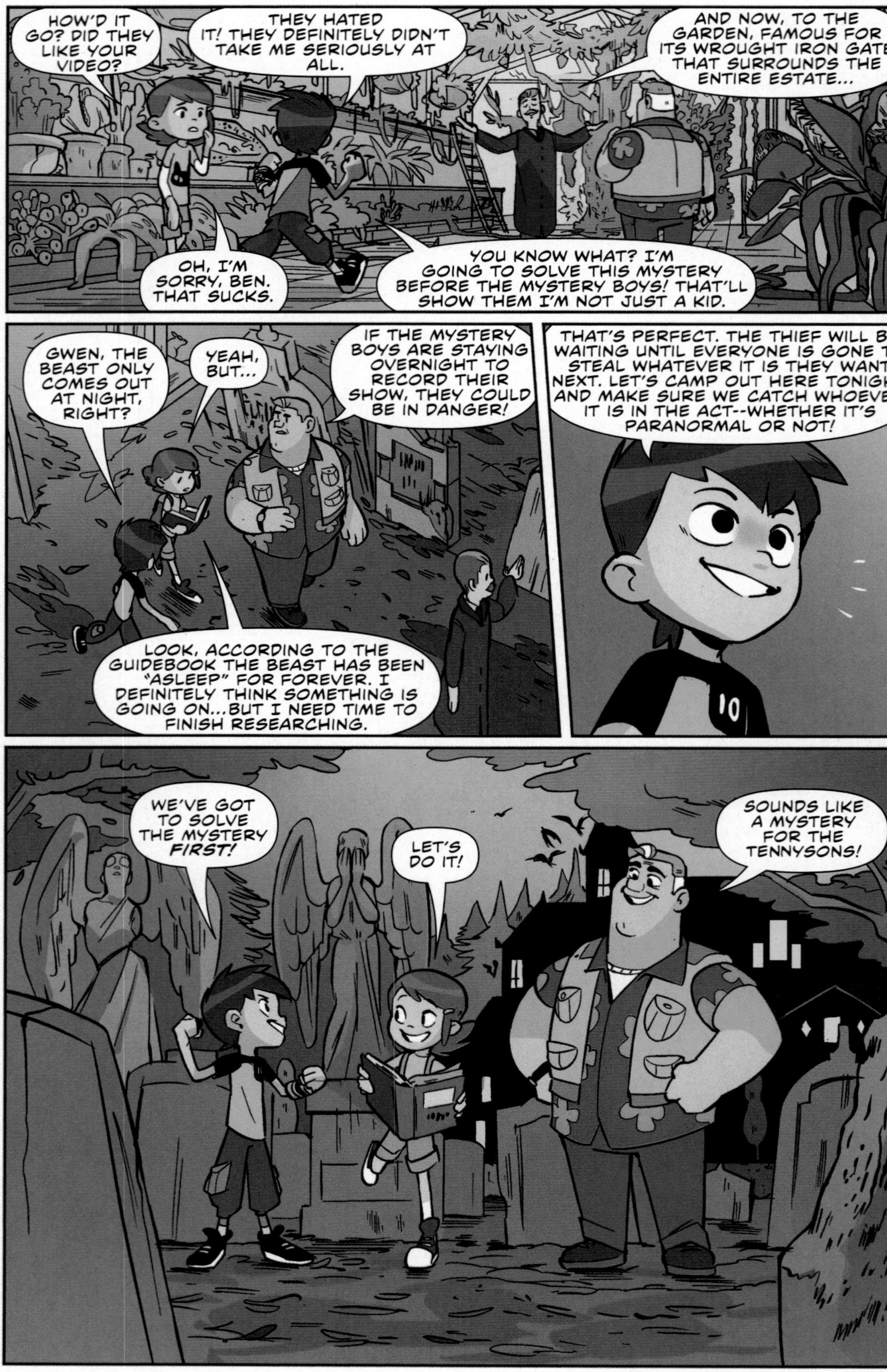
HOW'D IT GO? DID THEY LIKE YOUR VIDEO?
THEY HATED IT! THEY DEFINITELY DIDN'T TAKE ME SERIOUSLY AT ALL.
AND NOW, TO THE GARDEN, FAMOUS FOR ITS WROUGHT IRON GATE THAT SURROUNDS THE ENTIRE ESTATE...
OH, I'M SORRY, BEN. THAT SUCKS.
YOU KNOW WHAT? I'M GOING TO SOLVE THIS MYSTERY BEFORE THE MYSTERY BOYS! THAT'LL SHOW THEM I'M NOT JUST A KID.
GWEN, THE BEAST ONLY COMES OUT AT NIGHT, RIGHT?
YEAH, BUT...
IF THE MYSTERY BOYS ARE STAYING OVERNIGHT TO RECORD THEIR SHOW, THEY COULD BE IN DANGER!
LOOK, ACCORDING TO THE GUIDEBOOK THE BEAST HAS BEEN "ASLEEP" FOR FOREVER. I DEFINITELY THINK SOMETHING IS GOING ON...BUT I NEED TIME TO FINISH RESEARCHING.
THAT'S PERFECT. THE THIEF WILL BE WAITING UNTIL EVERYONE IS GONE TO STEAL WHATEVER IT IS THEY WANT NEXT. LET'S CAMP OUT HERE TONIGHT AND MAKE SURE WE CATCH WHOEVER IT IS IN THE ACT--WHETHER IT'S PARANORMAL OR NOT!
WE'VE GOT TO SOLVE THE MYSTERY *FIRST!*
LET'S DO IT!
SOUNDS LIKE A MYSTERY FOR THE TENNYSONS!

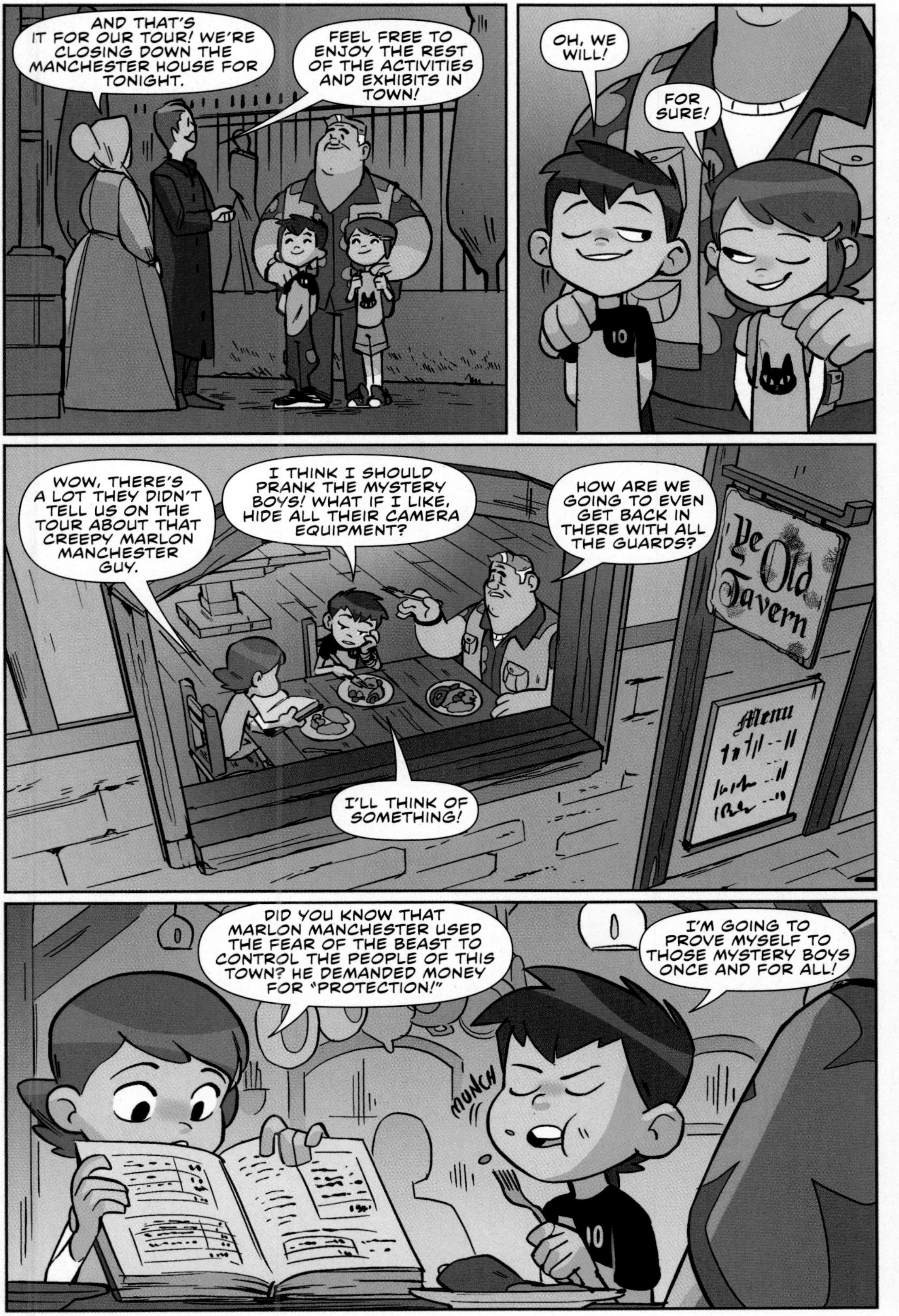
AND THAT'S IT FOR OUR TOUR! WE'RE CLOSING DOWN THE MANCHESTER HOUSE FOR TONIGHT.
FEEL FREE TO ENJOY THE REST OF THE ACTIVITIES AND EXHIBITS IN TOWN!
OH, WE WILL!
FOR SURE!
WOW, THERE'S A LOT THEY DIDN'T TELL US ON THE TOUR ABOUT THAT CREEPY MARLON MANCHESTER GUY.
I THINK I SHOULD PRANK THE MYSTERY BOYS! WHAT IF I LIKE, HIDE ALL THEIR CAMERA EQUIPMENT?
HOW ARE WE GOING TO EVEN GET BACK IN THERE WITH ALL THE GUARDS?
Ye Old Tavern
Menu
I'LL THINK OF SOMETHING!
DID YOU KNOW THAT MARLON MANCHESTER USED THE FEAR OF THE BEAST TO CONTROL THE PEOPLE OF THIS TOWN? HE DEMANDED MONEY FOR "PROTECTION!"
I'M GOING TO PROVE MYSELF TO THOSE MYSTERY BOYS ONCE AND FOR ALL!
MUNCH

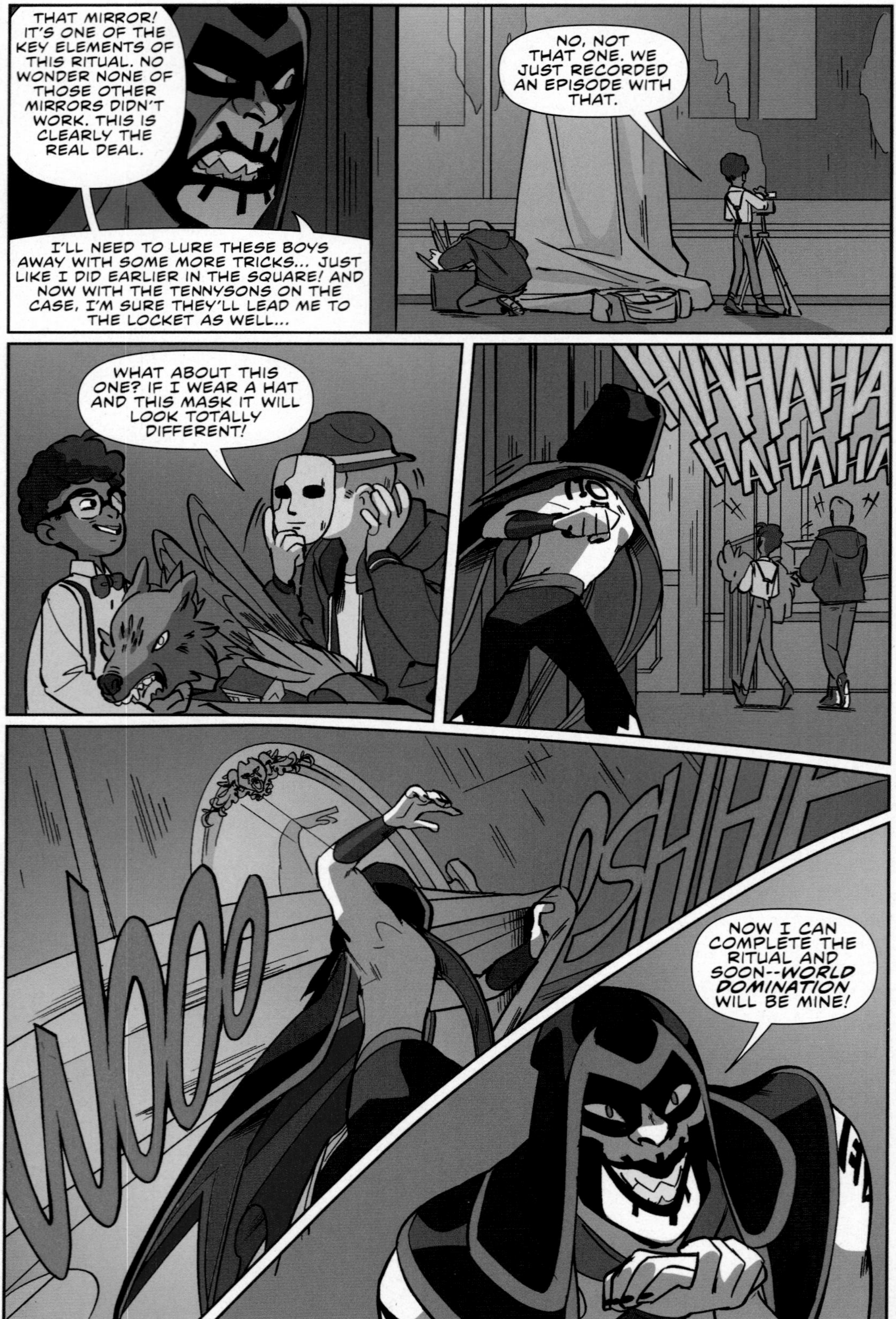
THAT MIRROR! IT'S ONE OF THE KEY ELEMENTS OF THIS RITUAL. NO WONDER NONE OF THOSE OTHER MIRRORS DIDN'T WORK. THIS IS CLEARLY THE REAL DEAL.
I'LL NEED TO LURE THESE BOYS AWAY WITH SOME MORE TRICKS... JUST LIKE I DID EARLIER IN THE SQUARE! AND NOW WITH THE TENNYSONS ON THE CASE, I'M SURE THEY'LL LEAD ME TO THE LOCKET AS WELL...
NO, NOT THAT ONE. WE JUST RECORDED AN EPISODE WITH THAT.
WHAT ABOUT THIS ONE? IF I WEAR A HAT AND THIS MASK IT WILL LOOK TOTALLY DIFFERENT!
HAHAHAHAHAHA
WOOOSHHH
NOW I CAN COMPLETE THE RITUAL AND SOON--*WORLD DOMINATION* WILL BE MINE!

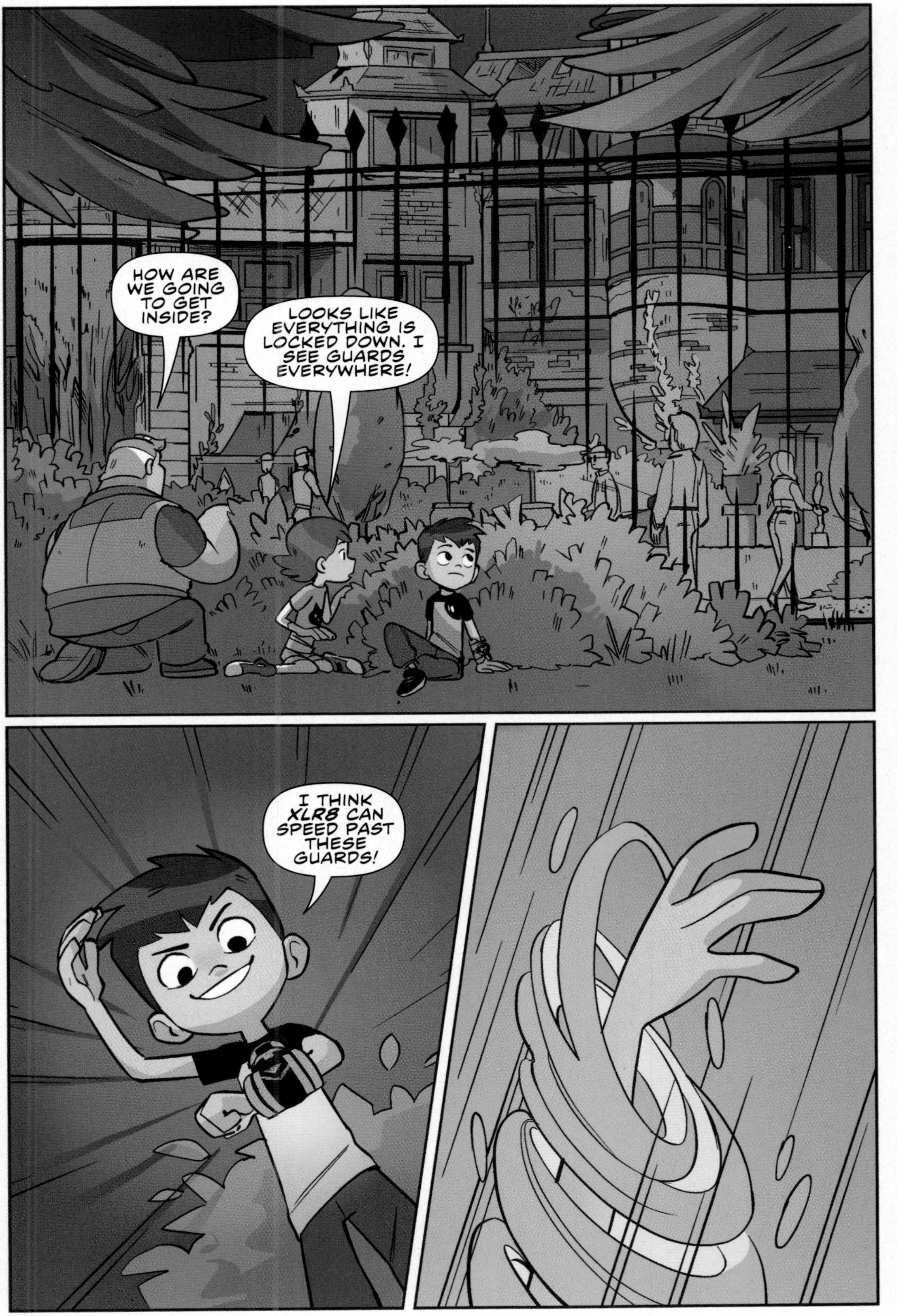
HOW ARE WE GOING TO GET INSIDE?
LOOKS LIKE EVERYTHING IS LOCKED DOWN. I SEE GUARDS EVERYWHERE!
I THINK *XLR8* CAN SPEED PAST THESE GUARDS!

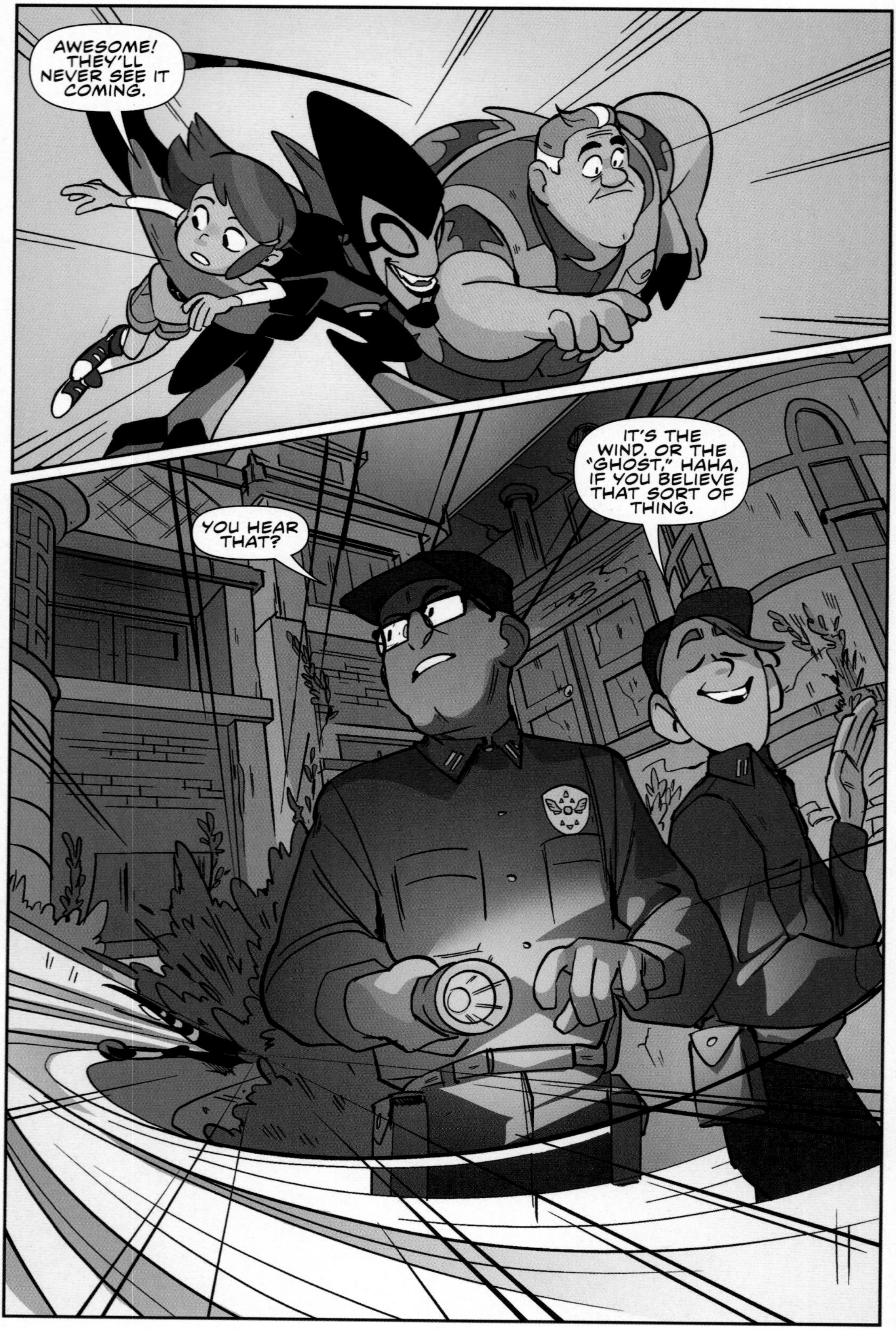
AWESOME! THEY'LL NEVER SEE IT COMING.
YOU HEAR THAT?
IT'S THE WIND. OR THE "GHOST," HAHA, IF YOU BELIEVE THAT SORT OF THING.

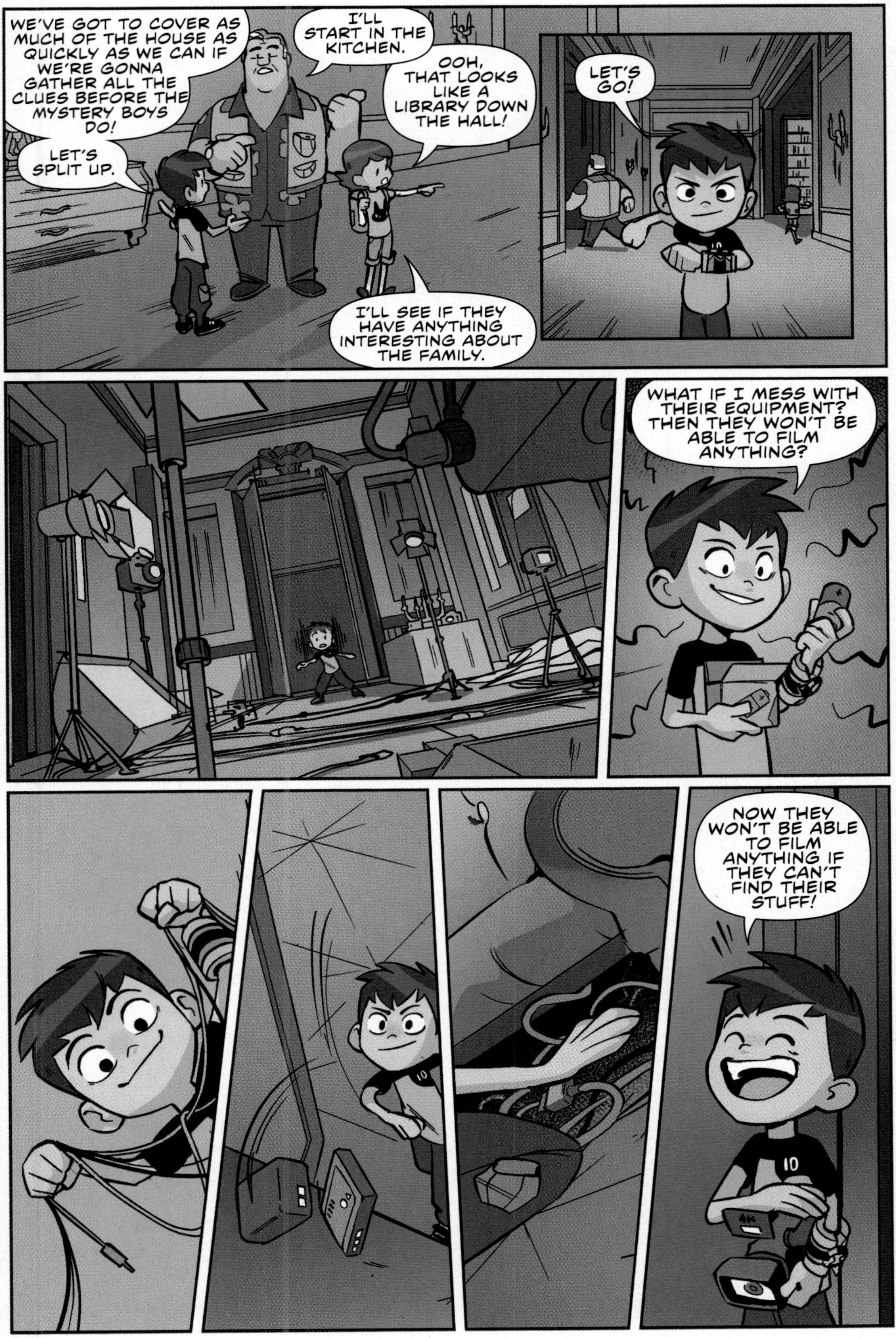
WE'VE GOT TO COVER AS MUCH OF THE HOUSE AS QUICKLY AS WE CAN IF WE'RE GONNA GATHER ALL THE CLUES BEFORE THE MYSTERY BOYS DO!
LET'S SPLIT UP.
I'LL START IN THE KITCHEN.
OOH, THAT LOOKS LIKE A LIBRARY DOWN THE HALL!
I'LL SEE IF THEY HAVE ANYTHING INTERESTING ABOUT THE FAMILY.
LET'S GO!
WHAT IF I MESS WITH THEIR EQUIPMENT? THEN THEY WON'T BE ABLE TO FILM ANYTHING?
NOW THEY WON'T BE ABLE TO FILM ANYTHING IF THEY CAN'T FIND THEIR STUFF!

WHAT ARE YOU DOING?

JUST A LITTLE HIDE-AND-SEEK FOR THE MYSTERY BOYS.

I THOUGHT OUR MISSION WAS TO CATCH THE THIEF AND INVESTIGATE THE CONNECTION WITH THE BEAST AND THE ITEMS.

OH, WE'RE GOING TO INVESTIGATE, ALL RIGHT! JUST NEED TO MAKE SURE WE GET THERE FIRST!

OH COME ON! THEY MIGHT JUST THINK IT'S A GHOST!

I DIDN'T SEE ANYTHING OF INTEREST IN THE KITCHEN. HOW ABOUT YOU TWO? GOT ANY CLUES SO FAR?

NOT IN THE LIVING ROOM OR THIS ONE! GWEN?

THE MANCHESTERS DEFINITELY WERE READERS. THEY HAD A LOT OF BOOKS, AND A FEW OF THEM WERE IN A SPECIAL DISPLAY. ONE OF THEM WAS MISSING...THE DIARY OF MARLON MANCHESTER.

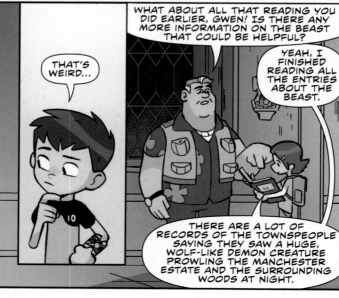

THAT'S WEIRD...

WHAT ABOUT ALL THAT READING YOU DID EARLIER, GWEN! IS THERE ANY MORE INFORMATION ON THE BEAST THAT COULD BE HELPFUL?

YEAH, I FINISHED READING ALL THE ENTRIES ABOUT THE BEAST.

THERE ARE A LOT OF RECORDS OF THE TOWNSPEOPLE SAYING THEY SAW A HUGE, WOLF-LIKE DEMON CREATURE PROWLING THE MANCHESTER ESTATE AND THE SURROUNDING WOODS AT NIGHT.

SO WHAT ARE WE LOOKING FOR EXACTLY? SOMETHING THAT BIG DOESN'T SEEM LIKE IT COULD HIDE IN THIS HOUSE.

IT SOUNDS LIKE PEOPLE SAW IT FADE AWAY INTO THE SHADOWS...THAT'S WHAT MUST HAVE STARTED THOSE STORIES OF IT BEING A "GHOST."

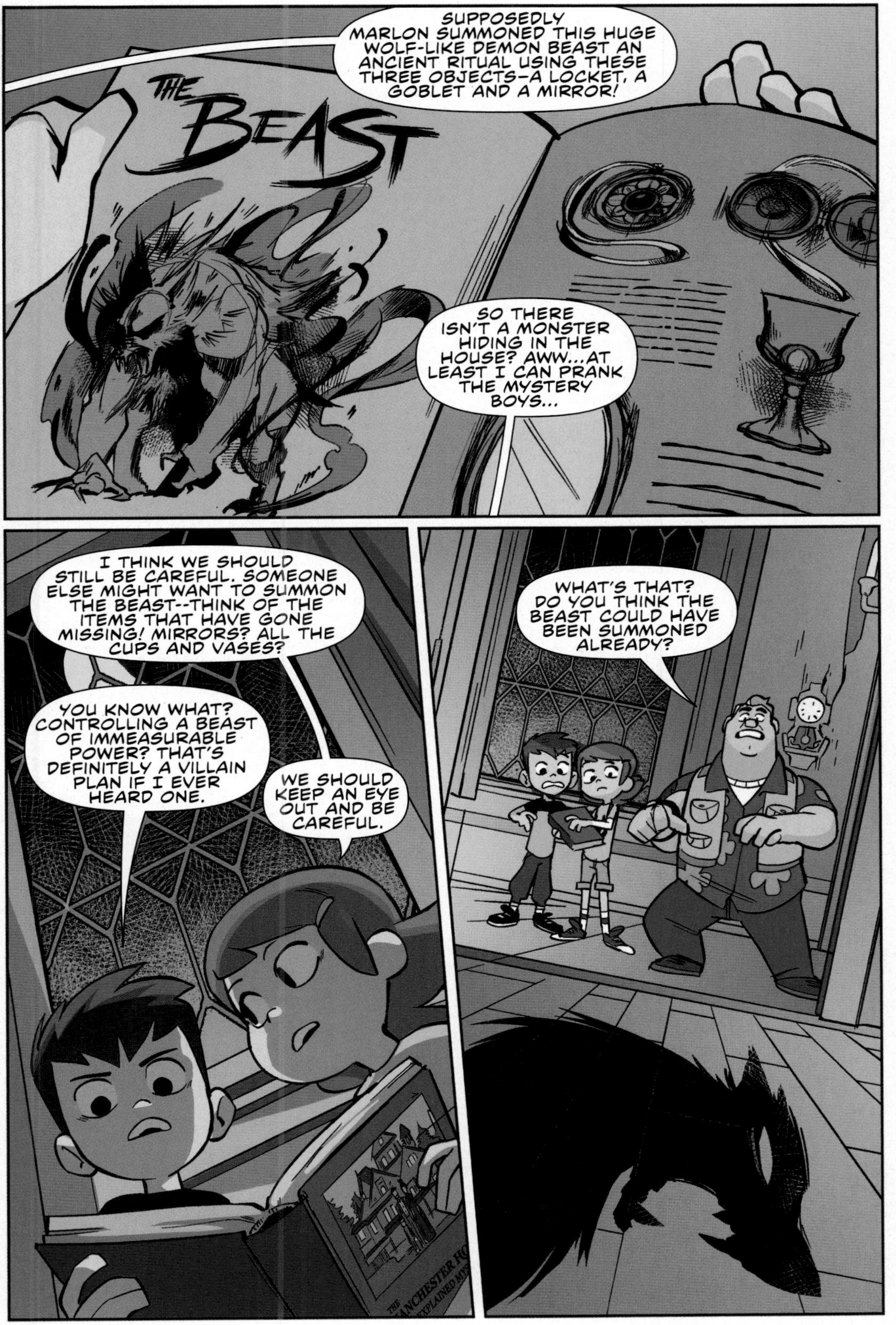
SUPPOSEDLY MARLON SUMMONED THIS HUGE WOLF-LIKE DEMON BEAST AN ANCIENT RITUAL USING THESE THREE OBJECTS–A LOCKET, A GOBLET AND A MIRROR!
THE BEAST
SO THERE ISN'T A MONSTER HIDING IN THE HOUSE? AWW...AT LEAST I CAN PRANK THE MYSTERY BOYS...
I THINK WE SHOULD STILL BE CAREFUL. SOMEONE ELSE MIGHT WANT TO SUMMON THE BEAST--THINK OF THE ITEMS THAT HAVE GONE MISSING! MIRRORS? ALL THE CUPS AND VASES?
YOU KNOW WHAT? CONTROLLING A BEAST OF IMMEASURABLE POWER? THAT'S DEFINITELY A VILLAIN PLAN IF I EVER HEARD ONE.
WE SHOULD KEEP AN EYE OUT AND BE CAREFUL.
WHAT'S THAT? DO YOU THINK THE BEAST COULD HAVE BEEN SUMMONED ALREADY?

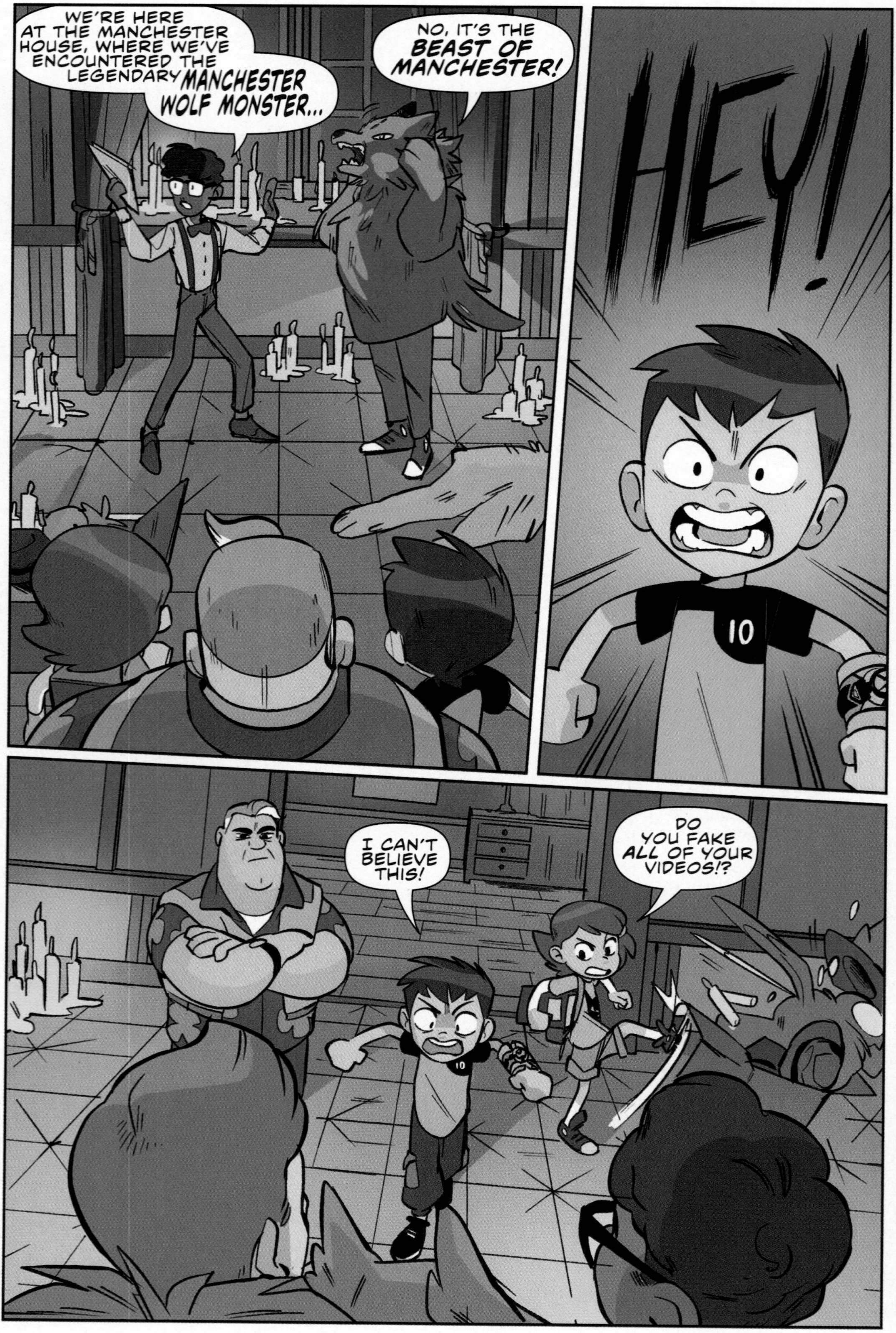
WE'RE HERE AT THE MANCHESTER HOUSE, WHERE WE'VE ENCOUNTERED THE LEGENDARY MANCHESTER WOLF MONSTER...
NO, IT'S THE BEAST OF MANCHESTER!
HEY!
10
I CAN'T BELIEVE THIS!
DO YOU FAKE ALL OF YOUR VIDEOS!?
10

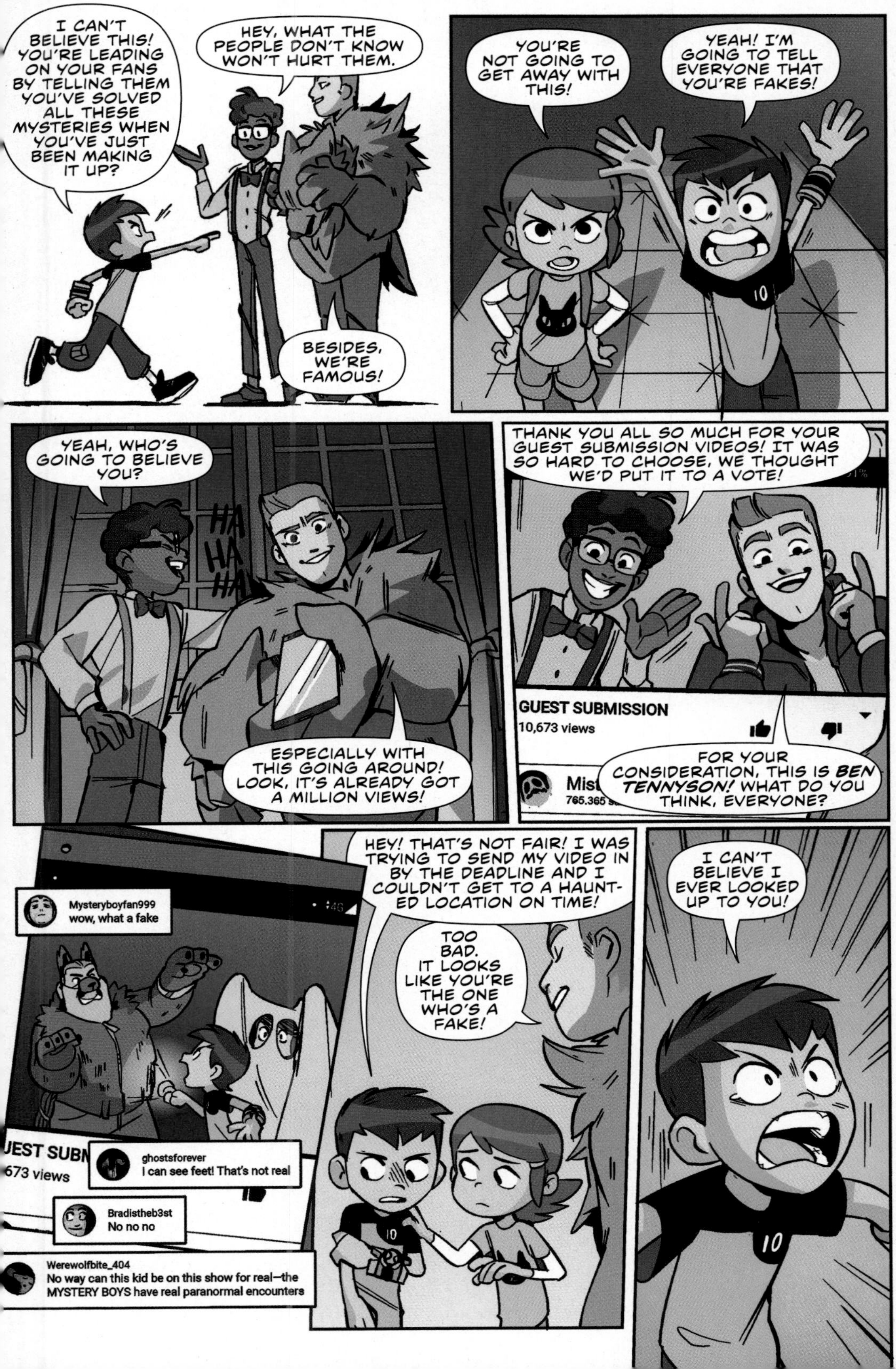
I CAN'T BELIEVE THIS! YOU'RE LEADING ON YOUR FANS BY TELLING THEM YOU'VE SOLVED ALL THESE MYSTERIES WHEN YOU'VE JUST BEEN MAKING IT UP?
HEY, WHAT THE PEOPLE DON'T KNOW WON'T HURT THEM.
BESIDES, WE'RE FAMOUS!
YOU'RE NOT GOING TO GET AWAY WITH THIS!
YEAH! I'M GOING TO TELL EVERYONE THAT YOU'RE FAKES!
10
YEAH, WHO'S GOING TO BELIEVE YOU?
HA HA HA
ESPECIALLY WITH THIS GOING AROUND! LOOK, IT'S ALREADY GOT A MILLION VIEWS!
THANK YOU ALL SO MUCH FOR YOUR GUEST SUBMISSION VIDEOS! IT WAS SO HARD TO CHOOSE, WE THOUGHT WE'D PUT IT TO A VOTE!
GUEST SUBMISSION
10,673 views
Mist
765.365
FOR YOUR CONSIDERATION, THIS IS BEN TENNYSON! WHAT DO YOU THINK, EVERYONE?
Mysteryboyfan999
wow, what a fake
UEST SUBM
673 views
ghostsforever
I can see feet! That's not real
Bradistheb3st
No no no
Werewolfbite_404
No way can this kid be on this show for real—the MYSTERY BOYS have real paranormal encounters
HEY! THAT'S NOT FAIR! I WAS TRYING TO SEND MY VIDEO IN BY THE DEADLINE AND I COULDN'T GET TO A HAUNTED LOCATION ON TIME!
TOO BAD. IT LOOKS LIKE YOU'RE THE ONE WHO'S A FAKE!
10
I CAN'T BELIEVE I EVER LOOKED UP TO YOU!
10

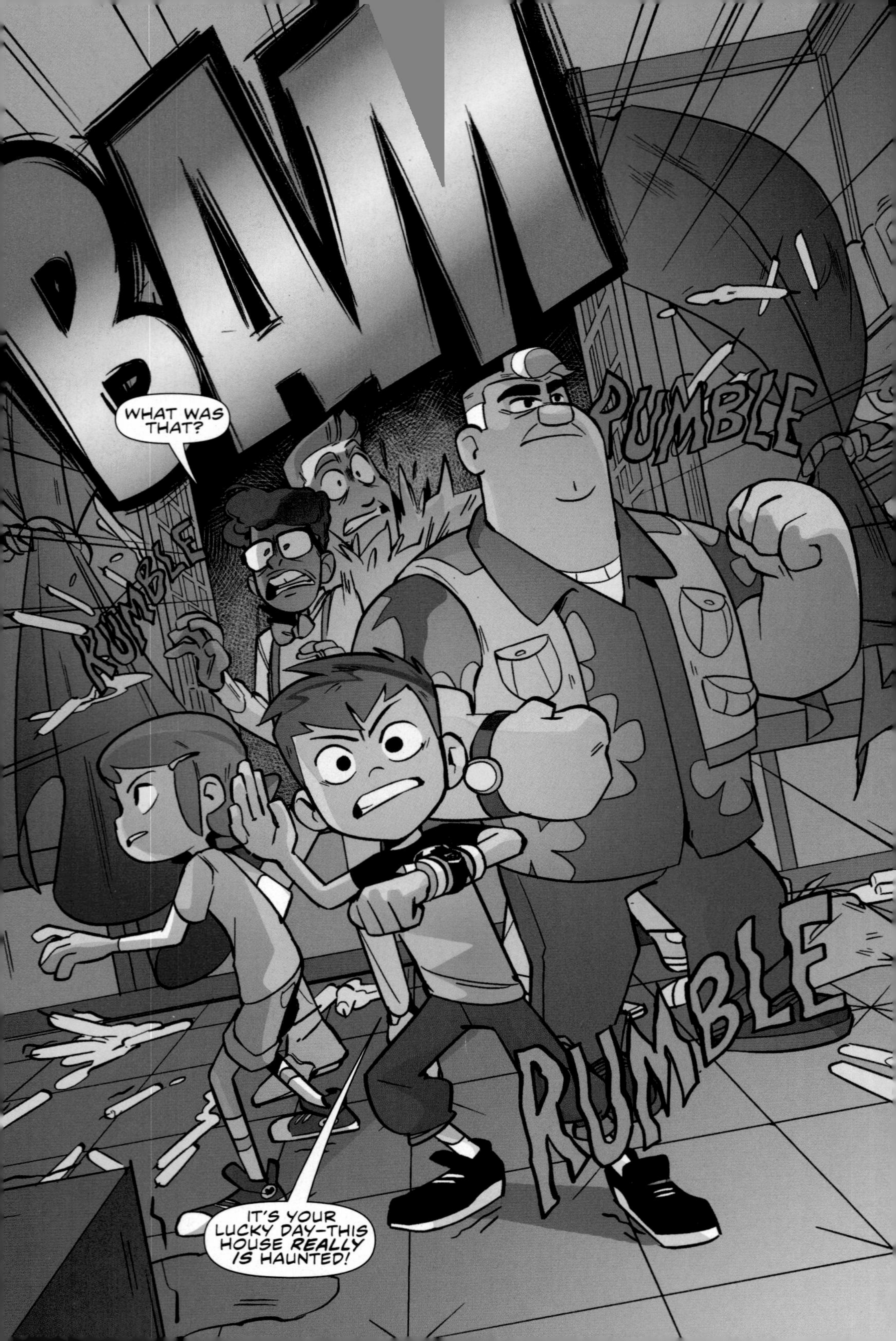
BAM!
WHAT WAS THAT?
RUMBLE
RUMBLE
RUMBLE
RUMBLE
IT'S YOUR LUCKY DAY–THIS HOUSE *REALLY IS* HAUNTED!

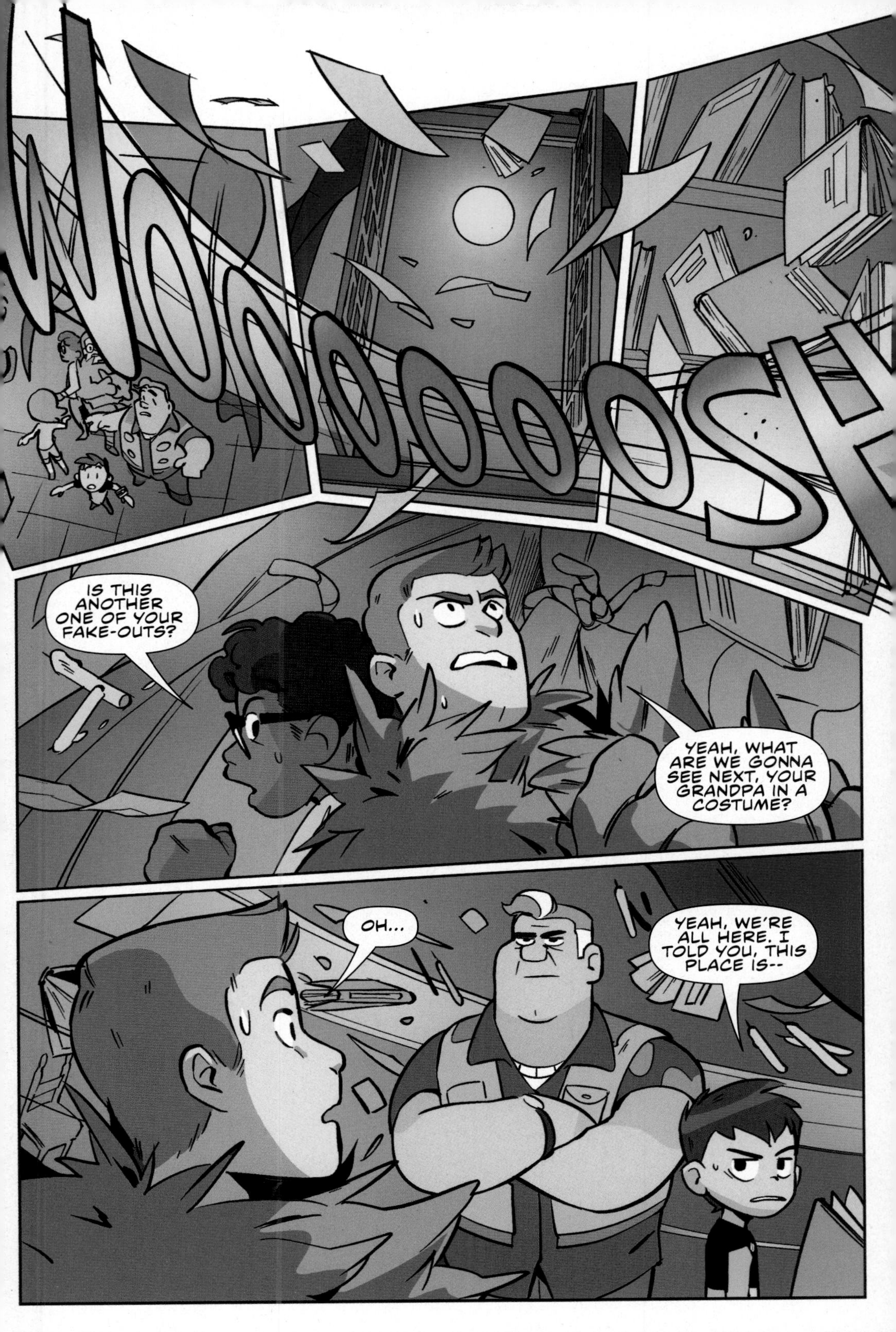
WOOOOOOOOOSH
IS THIS ANOTHER ONE OF YOUR FAKE-OUTS?
YEAH, WHAT ARE WE GONNA SEE NEXT, YOUR GRANDPA IN A COSTUME?
OH...
YEAH, WE'RE ALL HERE. I TOLD YOU, THIS PLACE IS--

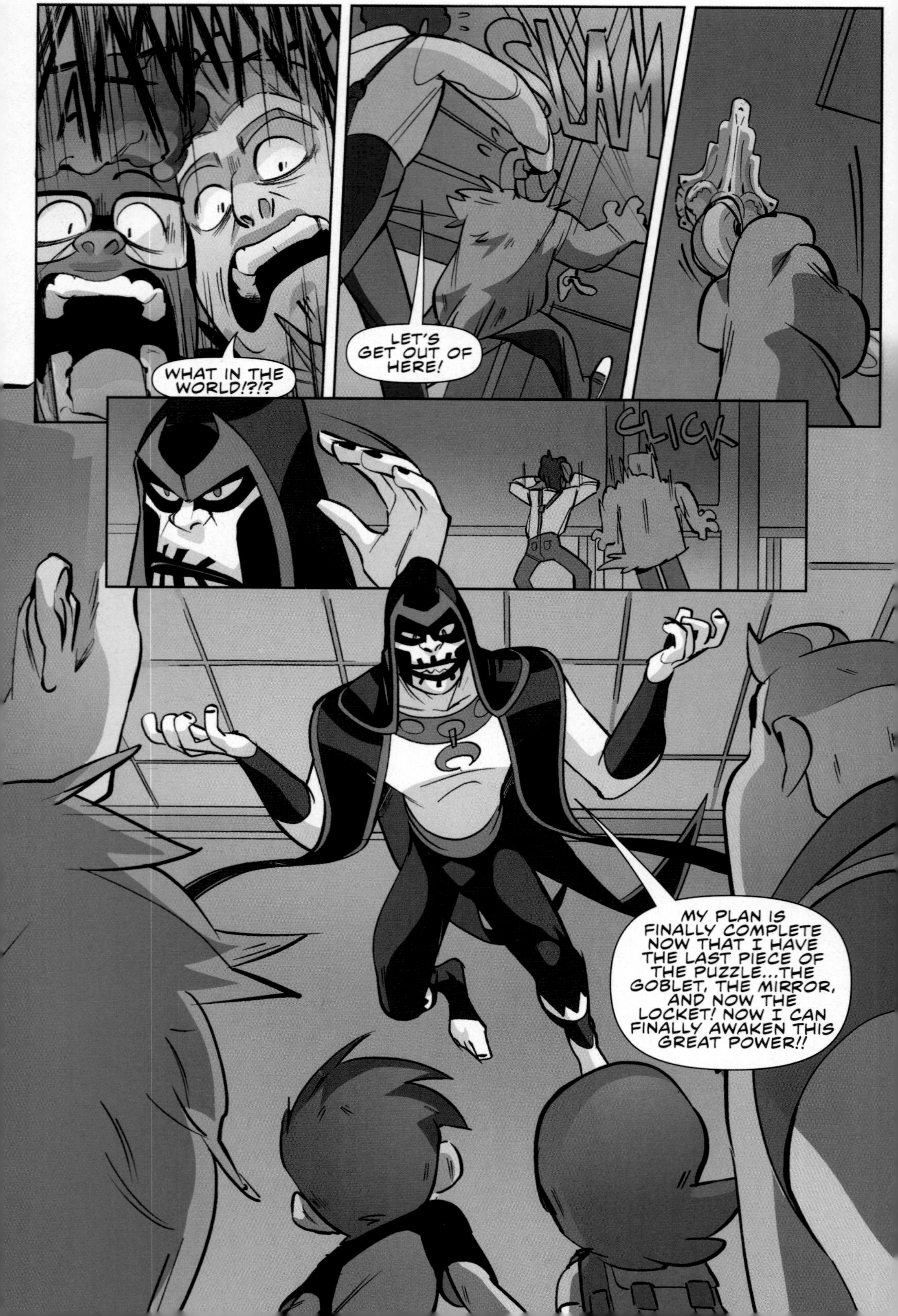
SLAM
WHAT IN THE WORLD!?!?
LET'S GET OUT OF HERE!
CLICK
MY PLAN IS FINALLY COMPLETE NOW THAT I HAVE THE LAST PIECE OF THE PUZZLE...THE GOBLET, THE MIRROR, AND NOW THE LOCKET! NOW I CAN FINALLY AWAKEN THIS GREAT POWER!!

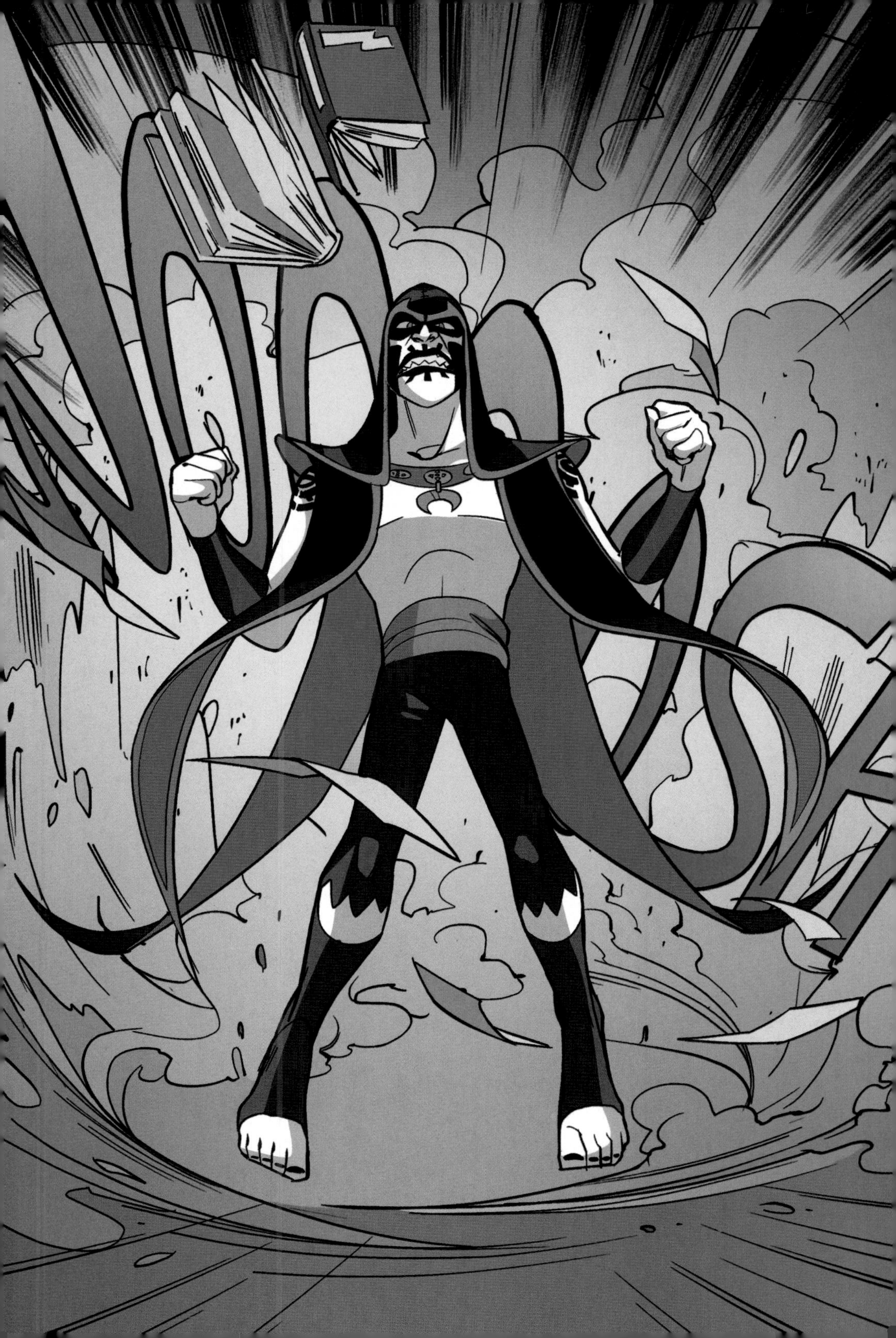

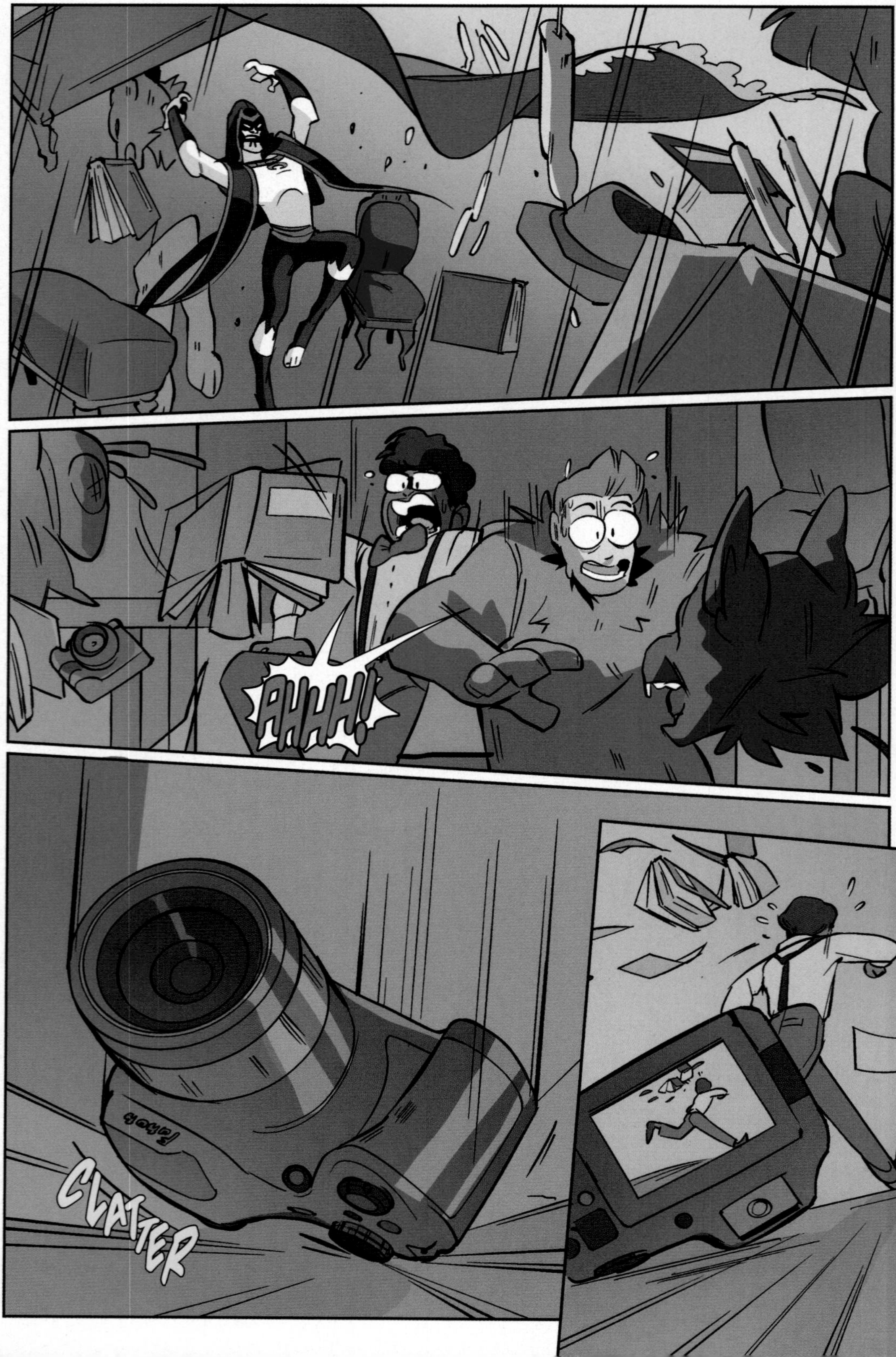
AHHH!
CLATTER

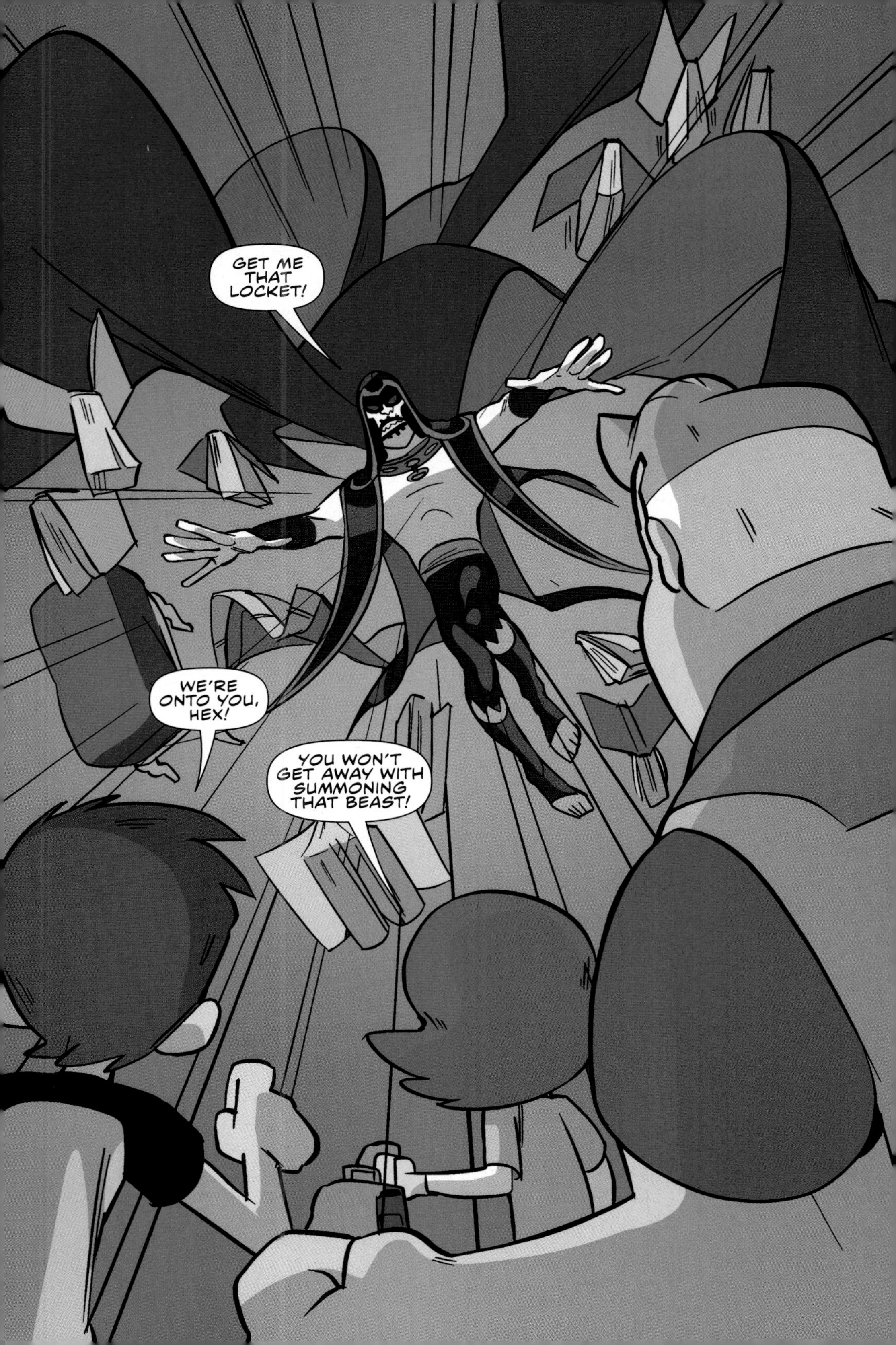
GET ME THAT LOCKET!
WE'RE ONTO YOU, HEX!
YOU WON'T GET AWAY WITH SUMMONING THAT BEAST!

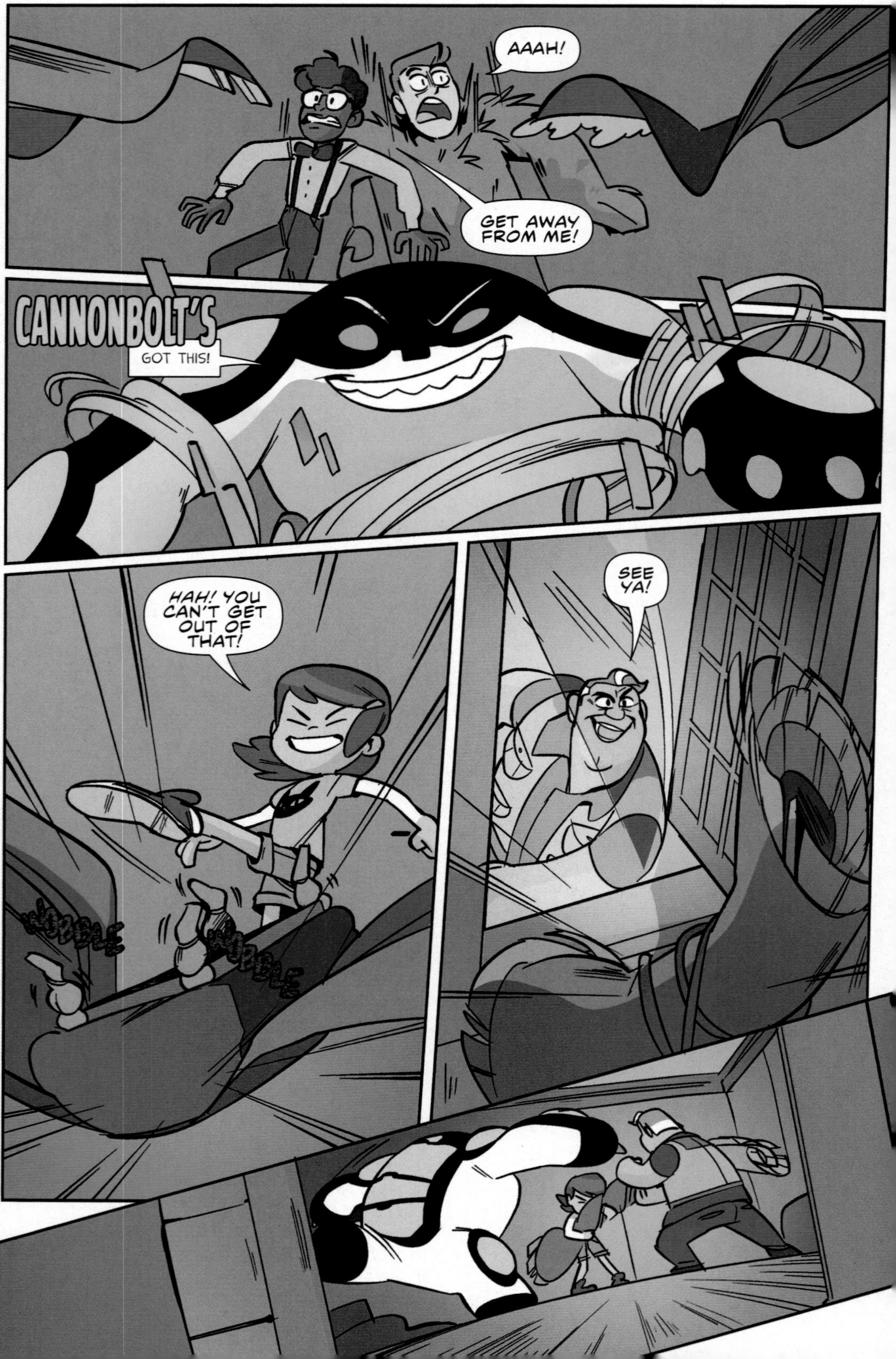
AAAH!
GET AWAY FROM ME!
CANNONBOLT'S
GOT THIS!
HAH! YOU CAN'T GET OUT OF THAT!
SEE YA!

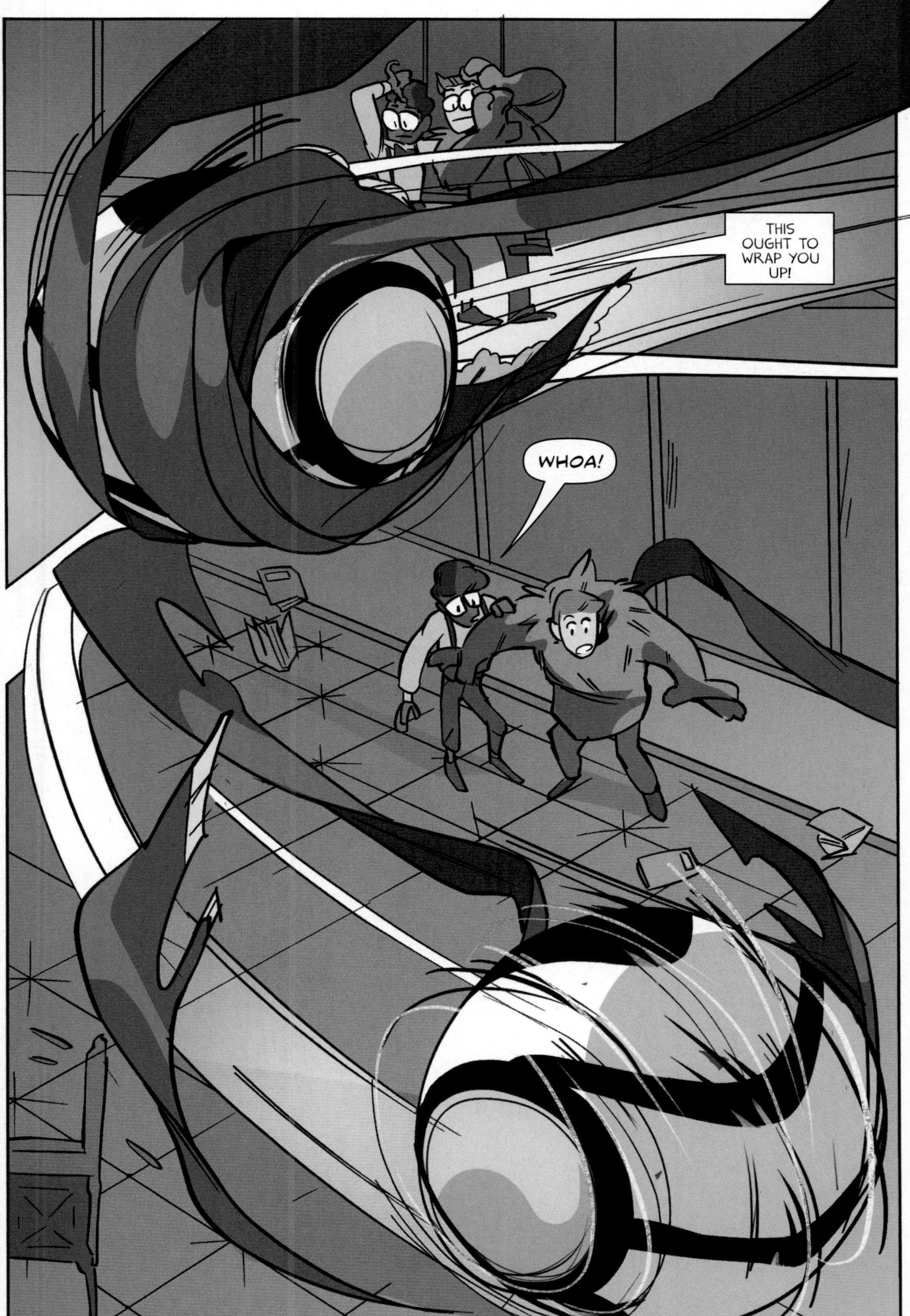
THIS OUGHT TO WRAP YOU UP!
WHOA!

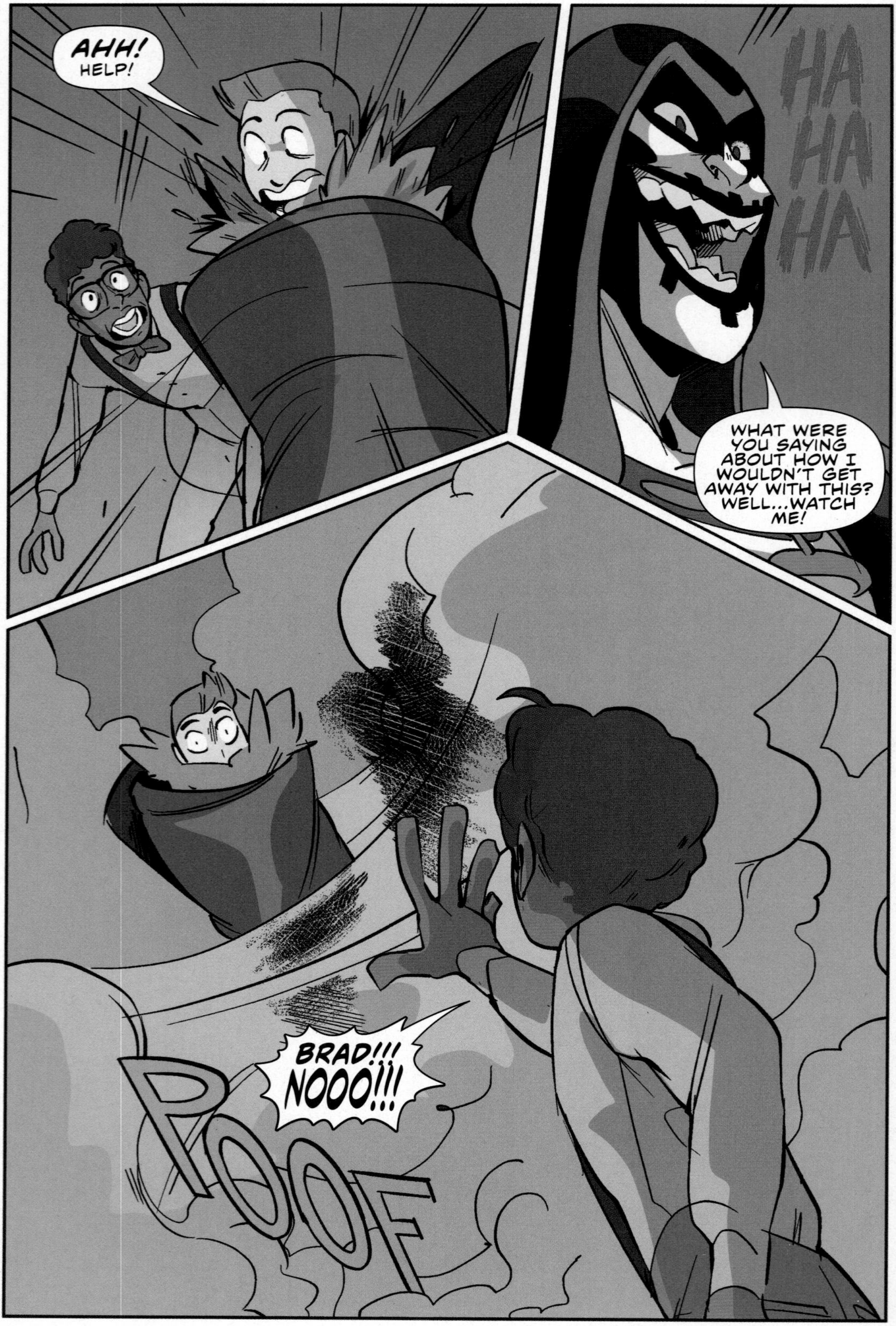
AHH! HELP!
HA HA HA HA
WHAT WERE YOU SAYING ABOUT HOW I WOULDN'T GET AWAY WITH THIS? WELL...WATCH ME!
BRAD!!! NOOO!!!
POOOF

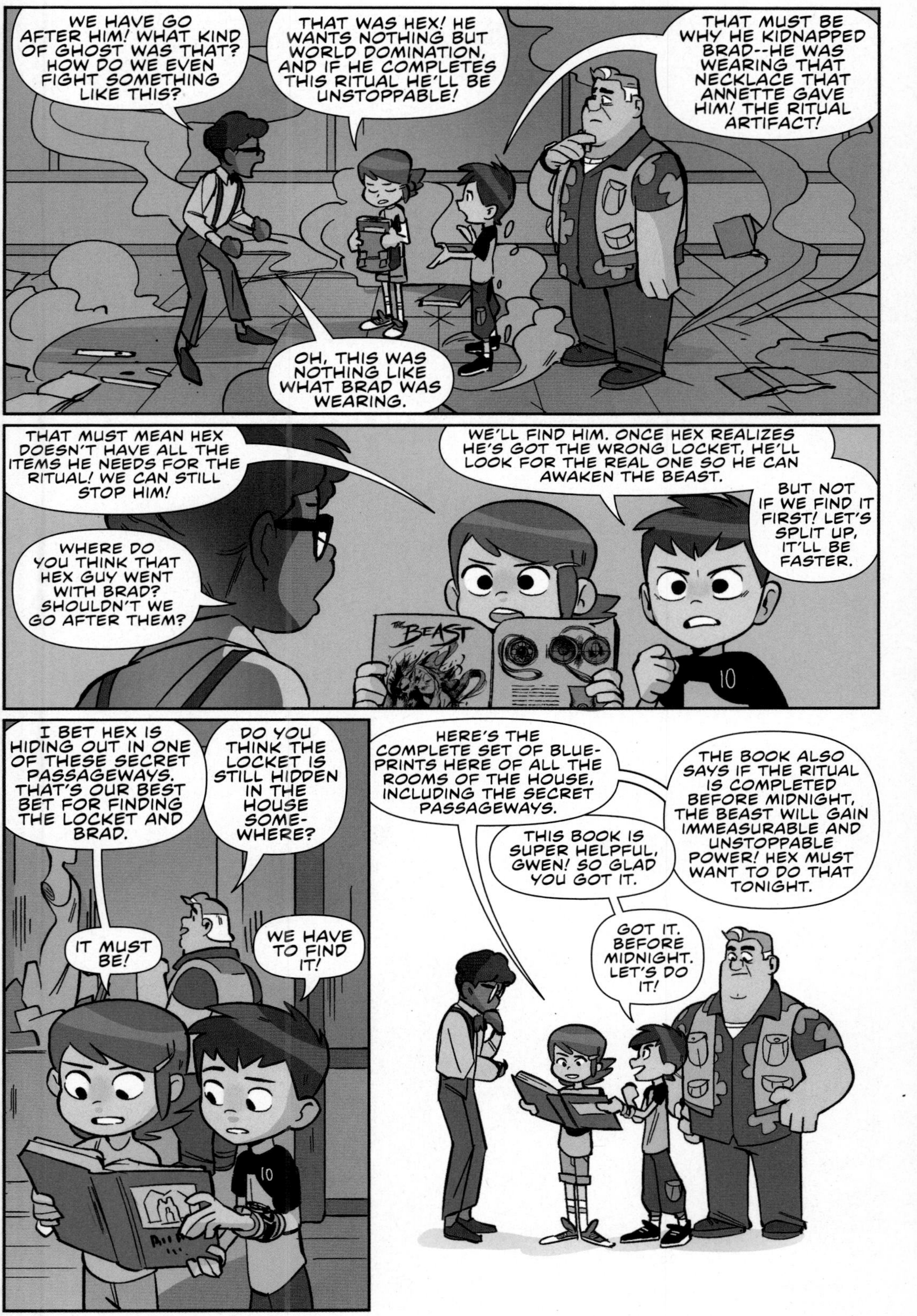
WE HAVE GO AFTER HIM! WHAT KIND OF GHOST WAS THAT? HOW DO WE EVEN FIGHT SOMETHING LIKE THIS?
THAT WAS HEX! HE WANTS NOTHING BUT WORLD DOMINATION, AND IF HE COMPLETES THIS RITUAL HE'LL BE UNSTOPPABLE!
THAT MUST BE WHY HE KIDNAPPED BRAD--HE WAS WEARING THAT NECKLACE THAT ANNETTE GAVE HIM! THE RITUAL ARTIFACT!
OH, THIS WAS NOTHING LIKE WHAT BRAD WAS WEARING.
THAT MUST MEAN HEX DOESN'T HAVE ALL THE ITEMS HE NEEDS FOR THE RITUAL! WE CAN STILL STOP HIM!
WHERE DO YOU THINK THAT HEX GUY WENT WITH BRAD? SHOULDN'T WE GO AFTER THEM?
WE'LL FIND HIM. ONCE HEX REALIZES HE'S GOT THE WRONG LOCKET, HE'LL LOOK FOR THE REAL ONE SO HE CAN AWAKEN THE BEAST.
BUT NOT IF WE FIND IT FIRST! LET'S SPLIT UP, IT'LL BE FASTER.
THE BEAST
I BET HEX IS HIDING OUT IN ONE OF THESE SECRET PASSAGEWAYS. THAT'S OUR BEST BET FOR FINDING THE LOCKET AND BRAD.
DO YOU THINK THE LOCKET IS STILL HIDDEN IN THE HOUSE SOME-WHERE?
IT MUST BE!
WE HAVE TO FIND IT!
HERE'S THE COMPLETE SET OF BLUE-PRINTS HERE OF ALL THE ROOMS OF THE HOUSE, INCLUDING THE SECRET PASSAGEWAYS.
THIS BOOK IS SUPER HELPFUL, GWEN! SO GLAD YOU GOT IT.
THE BOOK ALSO SAYS IF THE RITUAL IS COMPLETED BEFORE MIDNIGHT, THE BEAST WILL GAIN IMMEASURABLE AND UNSTOPPABLE POWER! HEX MUST WANT TO DO THAT TONIGHT.
GOT IT. BEFORE MIDNIGHT. LET'S DO IT!

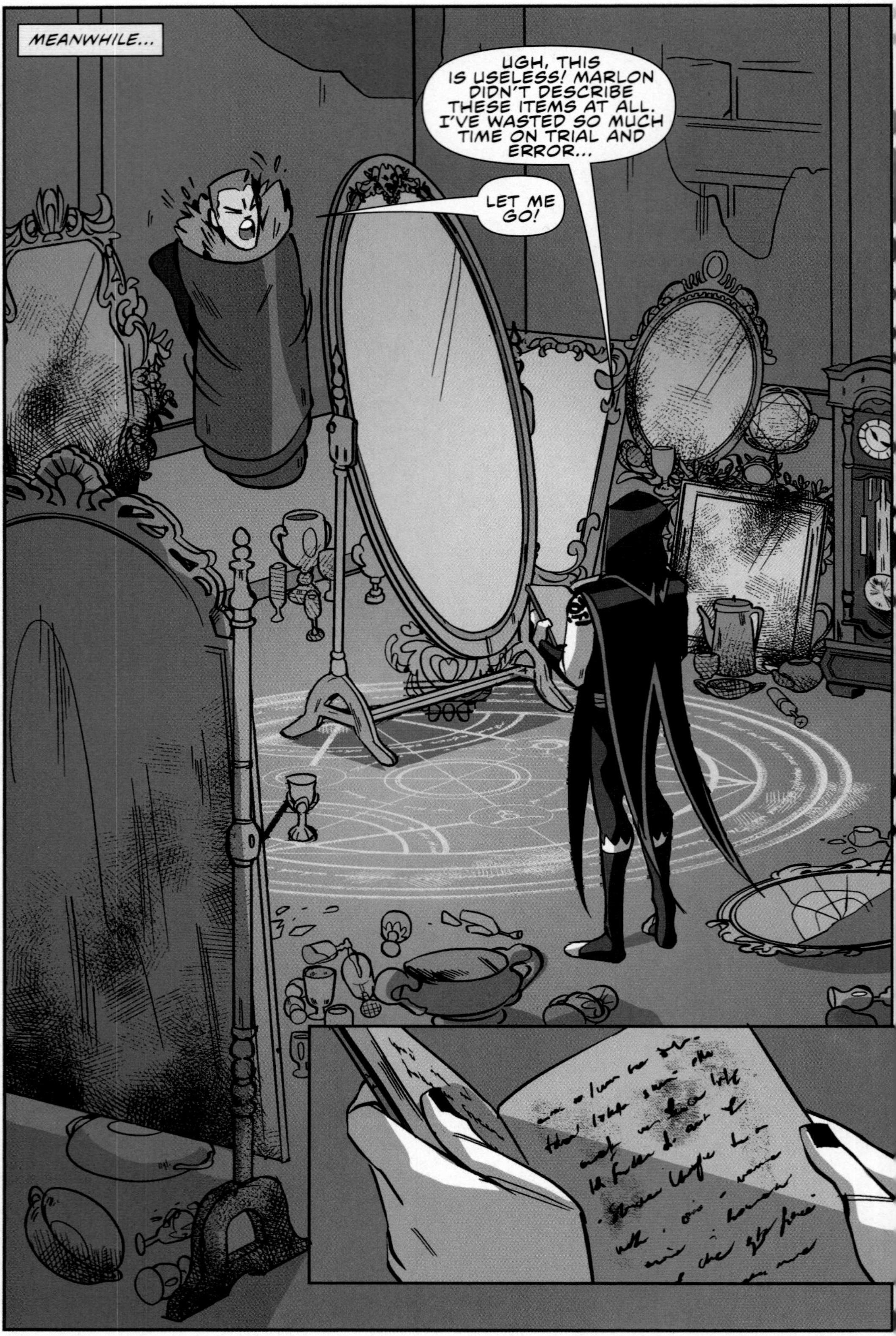
MEANWHILE...
LET ME GO!
UGH, THIS IS USELESS! MARLON DIDN'T DESCRIBE THESE ITEMS AT ALL. I'VE WASTED SO MUCH TIME ON TRIAL AND ERROR...

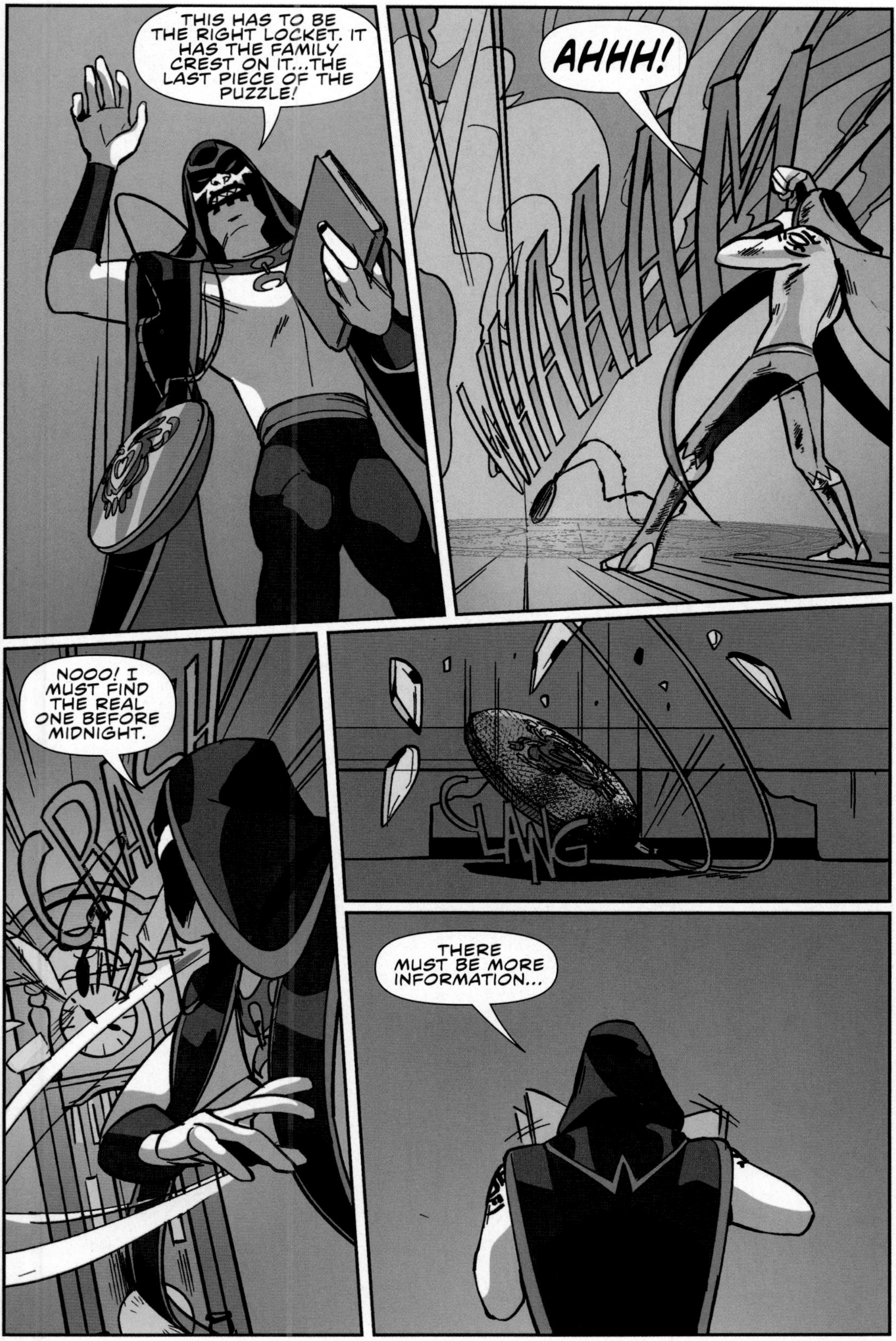
THIS HAS TO BE THE RIGHT LOCKET. IT HAS THE FAMILY CREST ON IT...THE LAST PIECE OF THE PUZZLE!
AHHH!
WHAAAAM
NOOO! I MUST FIND THE REAL ONE BEFORE MIDNIGHT.
CLANG
THERE MUST BE MORE INFORMATION...

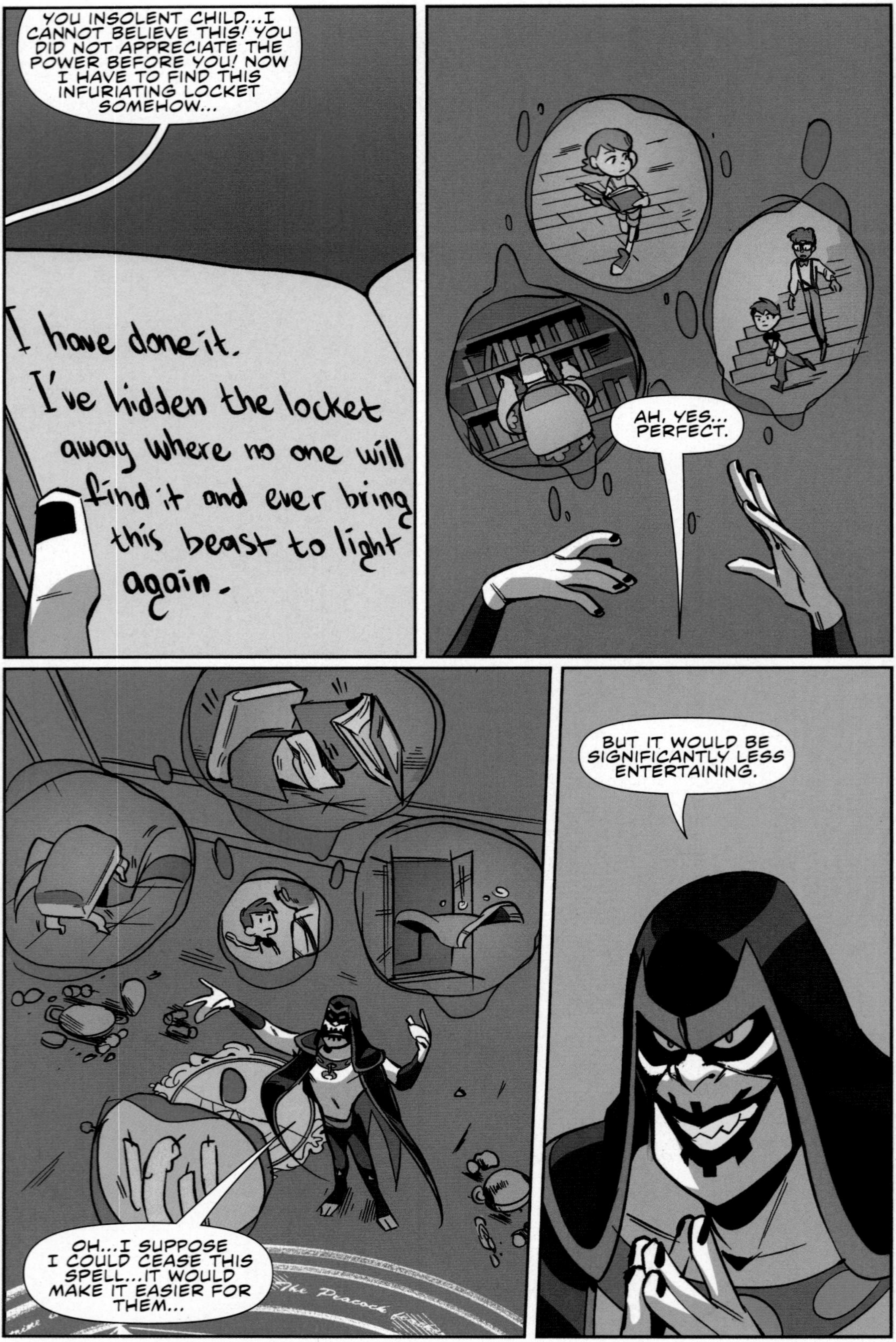
YOU INSOLENT CHILD...I CANNOT BELIEVE THIS! YOU DID NOT APPRECIATE THE POWER BEFORE YOU! NOW I HAVE TO FIND THIS INFURIATING LOCKET SOMEHOW...
I have done it. I've hidden the locket away where no one will find it and ever bring this beast to light again.
AH, YES... PERFECT.
OH...I SUPPOSE I COULD CEASE THIS SPELL...IT WOULD MAKE IT EASIER FOR THEM...
BUT IT WOULD BE SIGNIFICANTLY LESS ENTERTAINING.

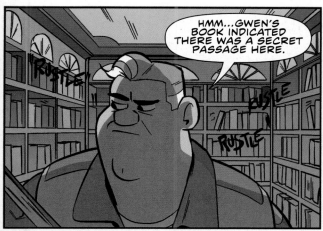

HMM...GWEN'S BOOK INDICATED THERE WAS A SECRET PASSAGE HERE.

RUSTLE RUSTLE RUSTLE RUSTLE

CLICK

AHA!

NO HEX...

SCROLL

NO LOCKET EITHER-- WHOA!

THAT OUGHT TO HOLD YOU!

SLAM

THUMP THUMP

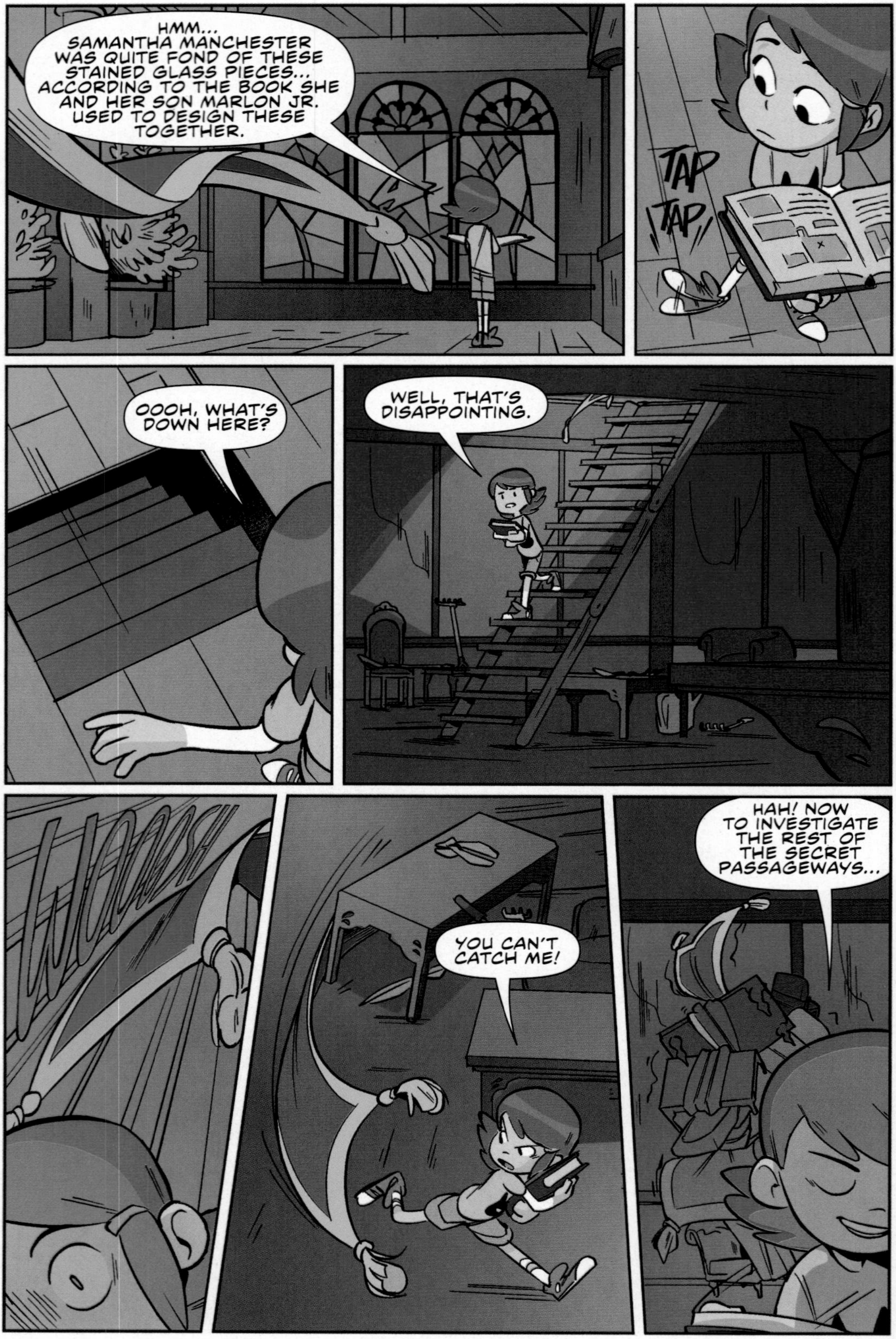
HMM... SAMANTHA MANCHESTER WAS QUITE FOND OF THESE STAINED GLASS PIECES... ACCORDING TO THE BOOK SHE AND HER SON MARLON JR. USED TO DESIGN THESE TOGETHER.
TAP
TAP
OOOH, WHAT'S DOWN HERE?
WELL, THAT'S DISAPPOINTING.
WOOSH
YOU CAN'T CATCH ME!
HAH! NOW TO INVESTIGATE THE REST OF THE SECRET PASSAGEWAYS...

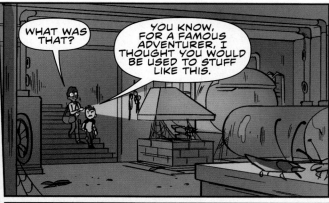

THERE'S A SECRET ROOM BEHIND THE BOILER ROOM DOWNSTAIRS.

DO YOU THINK MORE FURNITURE IS GOING TO ATTACK US?

WHAT WAS THAT?

YOU KNOW, FOR A FAMOUS ADVENTURER, I THOUGHT YOU WOULD BE USED TO STUFF LIKE THIS.

PROBABLY. THAT'S ONE OF HEX'S FAVORITE SPELLS, BRINGING INANIMATE OBJECTS TO LIFE.

YEAH, I'VE NEVER DONE ANYTHING LIKE THIS. THERE'S NEVER REALLY BEEN ANY DANGER...SINCE WE MAKE IT ALL UP.

UH HUH...

I'M SORRY WE PUT THAT VIDEO UP. BUT IT'S JUST THE BUSINESS, YOU KNOW? WE NEVER WERE GOING TO PICK GUEST, WE JUST WANTED THE VIEWERSHIP BUMP...

BUT YOU MADE SO MANY PEOPLE THINK THEY HAD A CHANCE! THAT ISN'T FAIR.

YOU'RE RIGHT.

TELL YOU WHAT, AFTER ALL THIS IS OVER, I PROMISE WE'LL COME CLEAN ABOUT THE SHOW. AND WE'LL FOCUS ON REAL ADVENTURES, LIKE THIS!

AND YOU SHOULD COME BE A GUEST STAR! SHOW US WHAT ADVENTURE IS REALLY ABOUT.

HMM, MAYBE... WAIT--WHAT'S THAT?

THERE'S AN EDGE HERE...THIS MUST BE ONE OF THE SECRET PASSAGEWAYS...

WHOA... WAIT, DO YOU HEAR THAT?

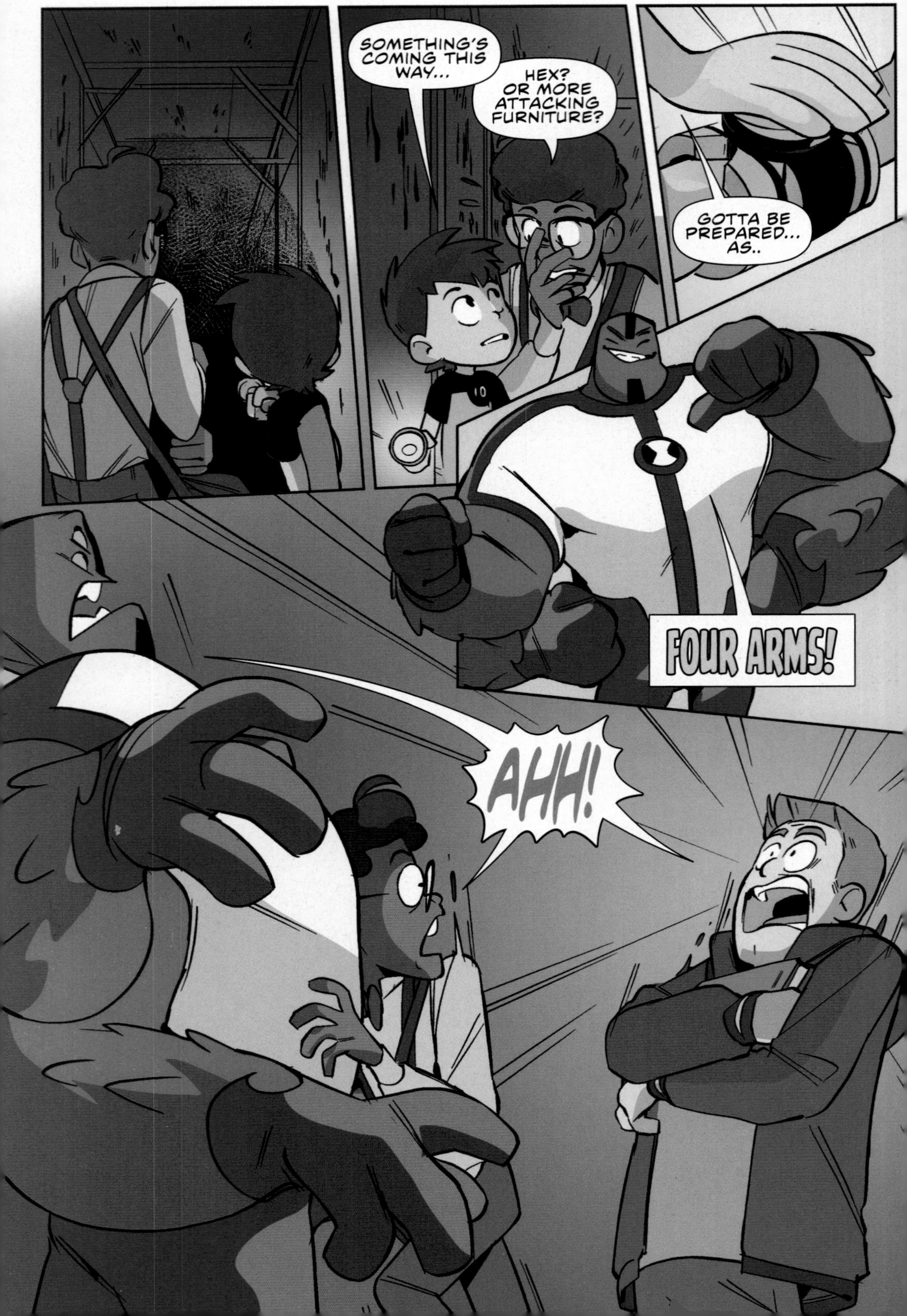
SOMETHING'S COMING THIS WAY...
HEX? OR MORE ATTACKING FURNITURE?
GOTTA BE PREPARED... AS..
FOUR ARMS!
AHH!

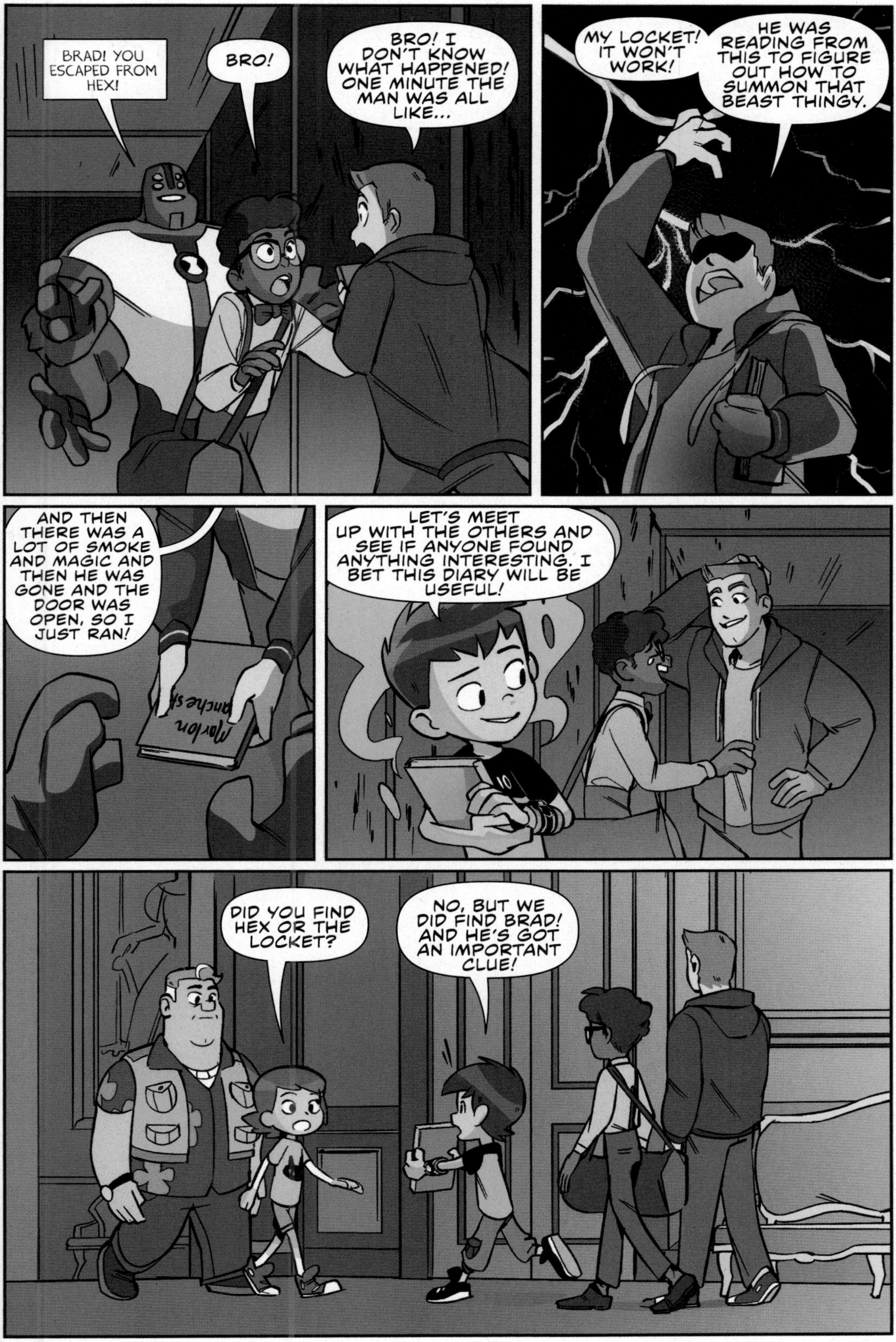
BRAD! YOU ESCAPED FROM HEX!
BRO!
BRO! I DON'T KNOW WHAT HAPPENED! ONE MINUTE THE MAN WAS ALL LIKE...
MY LOCKET! IT WON'T WORK!
HE WAS READING FROM THIS TO FIGURE OUT HOW TO SUMMON THAT BEAST THINGY.
AND THEN THERE WAS A LOT OF SMOKE AND MAGIC AND THEN HE WAS GONE AND THE DOOR WAS OPEN, SO I JUST RAN!
LET'S MEET UP WITH THE OTHERS AND SEE IF ANYONE FOUND ANYTHING INTERESTING. I BET THIS DIARY WILL BE USEFUL!
DID YOU FIND HEX OR THE LOCKET?
NO, BUT WE DID FIND BRAD! AND HE'S GOT AN IMPORTANT CLUE!

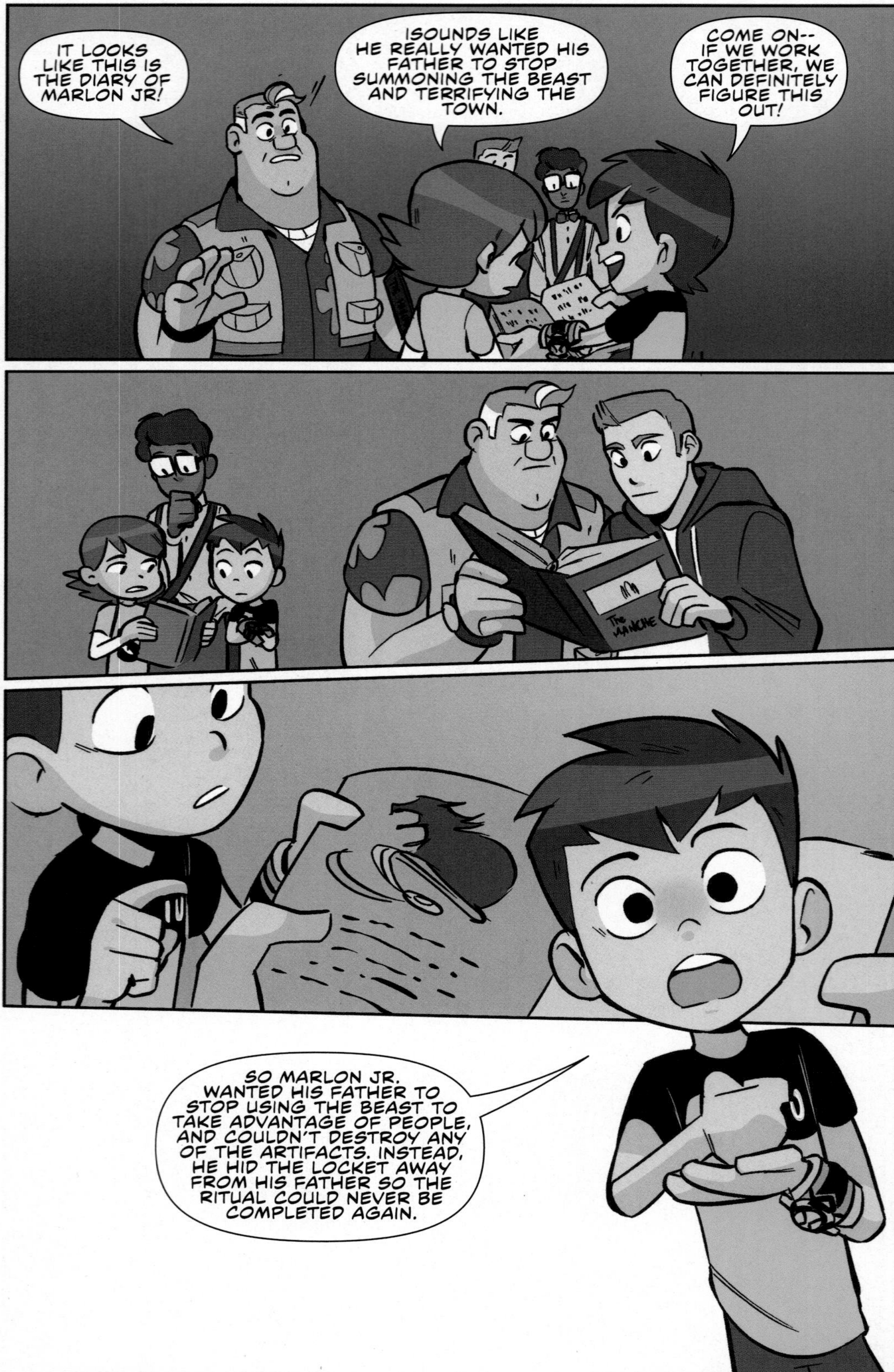
IT LOOKS LIKE THIS IS THE DIARY OF MARLON JR!
ISOUNDS LIKE HE REALLY WANTED HIS FATHER TO STOP SUMMONING THE BEAST AND TERRIFYING THE TOWN.
COME ON-- IF WE WORK TOGETHER, WE CAN DEFINITELY FIGURE THIS OUT!
SO MARLON JR. WANTED HIS FATHER TO STOP USING THE BEAST TO TAKE ADVANTAGE OF PEOPLE, AND COULDN'T DESTROY ANY OF THE ARTIFACTS. INSTEAD, HE HID THE LOCKET AWAY FROM HIS FATHER SO THE RITUAL COULD NEVER BE COMPLETED AGAIN.

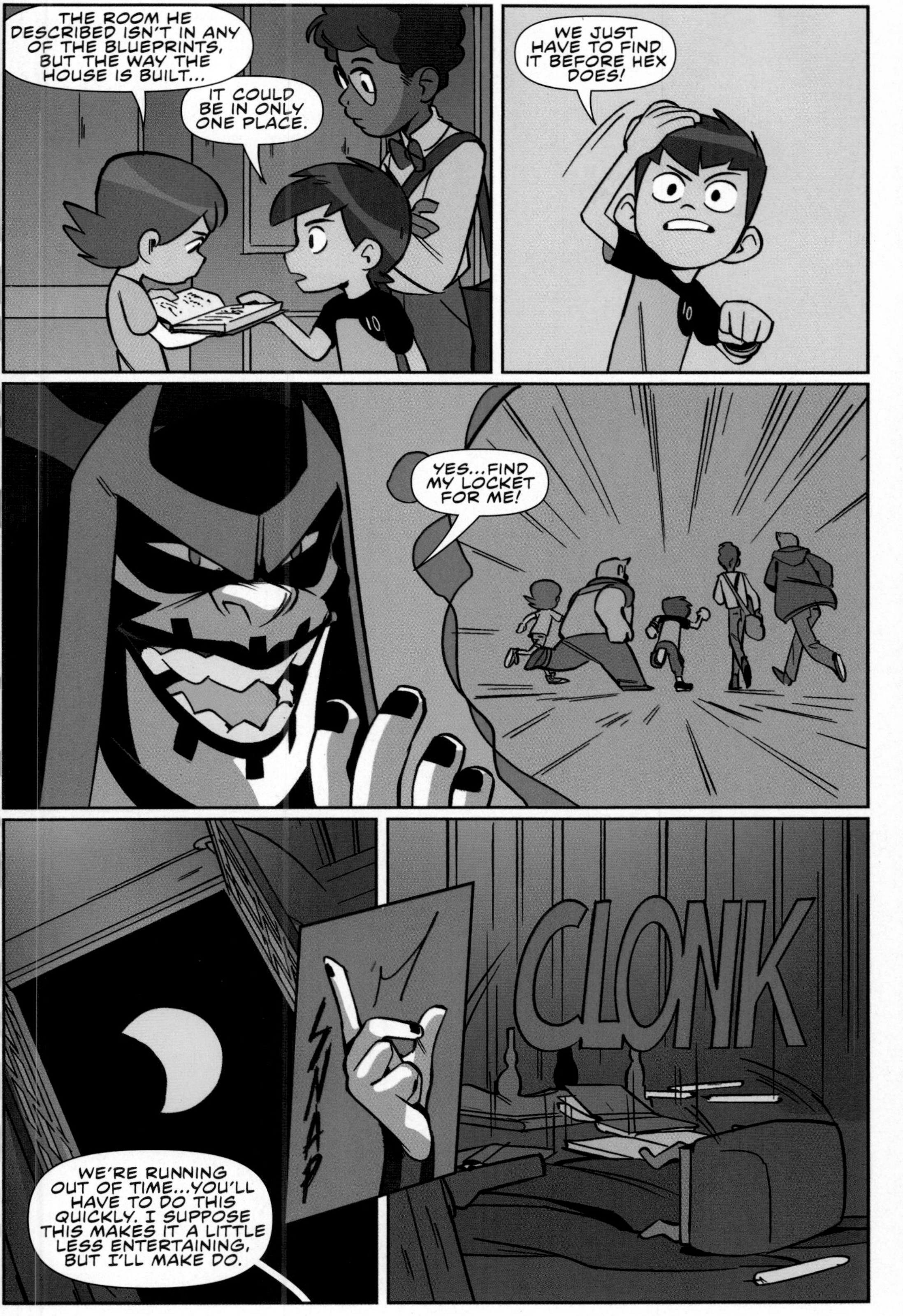
THE ROOM HE DESCRIBED ISN'T IN ANY OF THE BLUEPRINTS, BUT THE WAY THE HOUSE IS BUILT...
IT COULD BE IN ONLY ONE PLACE.
WE JUST HAVE TO FIND IT BEFORE HEX DOES!
YES...FIND MY LOCKET FOR ME!
WE'RE RUNNING OUT OF TIME...YOU'LL HAVE TO DO THIS QUICKLY. I SUPPOSE THIS MAKES IT A LITTLE LESS ENTERTAINING, BUT I'LL MAKE DO.
SNAP
CLONK

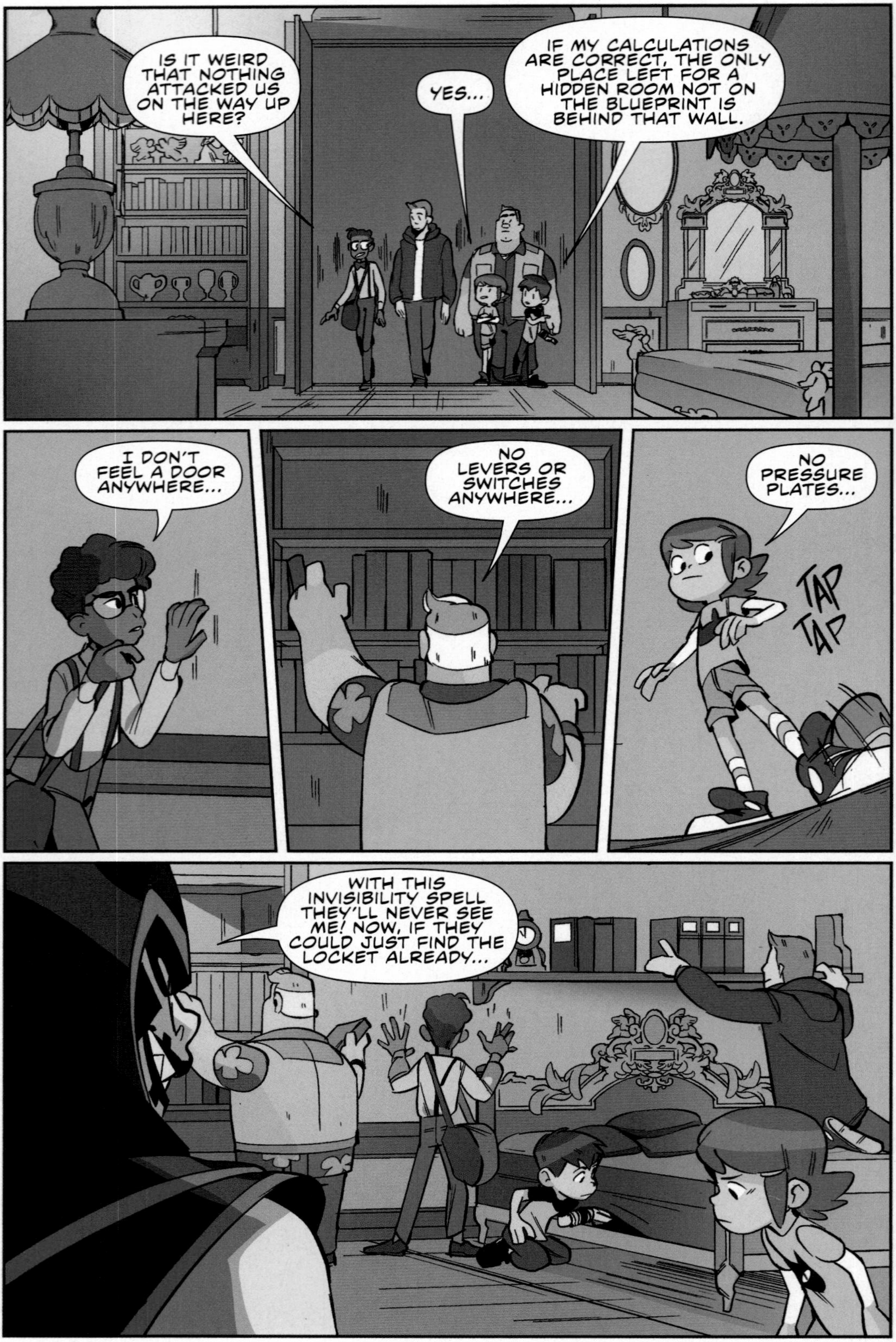
IS IT WEIRD THAT NOTHING ATTACKED US ON THE WAY UP HERE?
YES...
IF MY CALCULATIONS ARE CORRECT, THE ONLY PLACE LEFT FOR A HIDDEN ROOM NOT ON THE BLUEPRINT IS BEHIND THAT WALL.
I DON'T FEEL A DOOR ANYWHERE...
NO LEVERS OR SWITCHES ANYWHERE...
NO PRESSURE PLATES...
TAP TAP
WITH THIS INVISIBILITY SPELL THEY'LL NEVER SEE ME! NOW, IF THEY COULD JUST FIND THE LOCKET ALREADY...

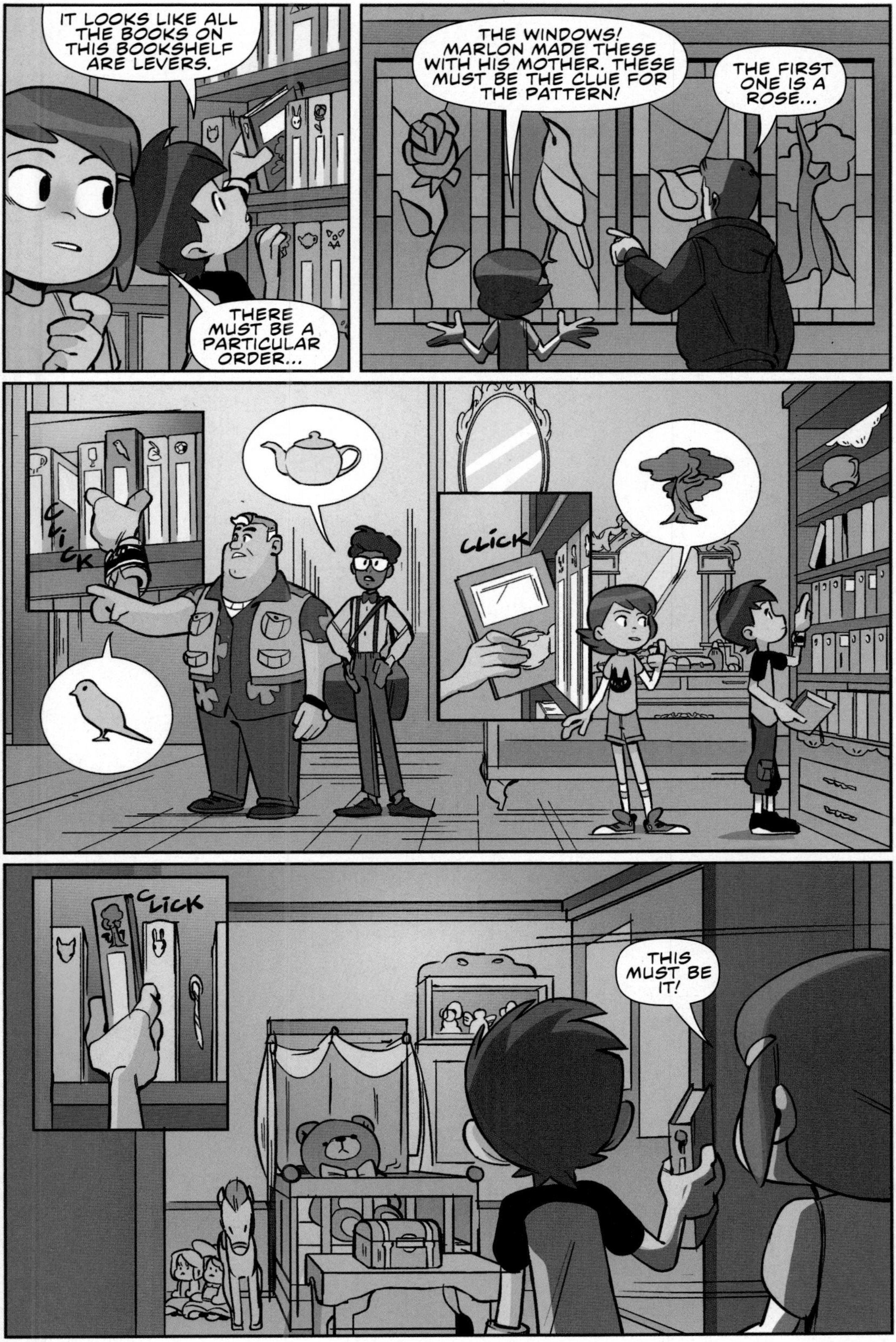
IT LOOKS LIKE ALL THE BOOKS ON THIS BOOKSHELF ARE LEVERS.
THERE MUST BE A PARTICULAR ORDER...
THE WINDOWS! MARLON MADE THESE WITH HIS MOTHER. THESE MUST BE THE CLUE FOR THE PATTERN!
THE FIRST ONE IS A ROSE...
CLICK
CLICK
CLICK
THIS MUST BE IT!

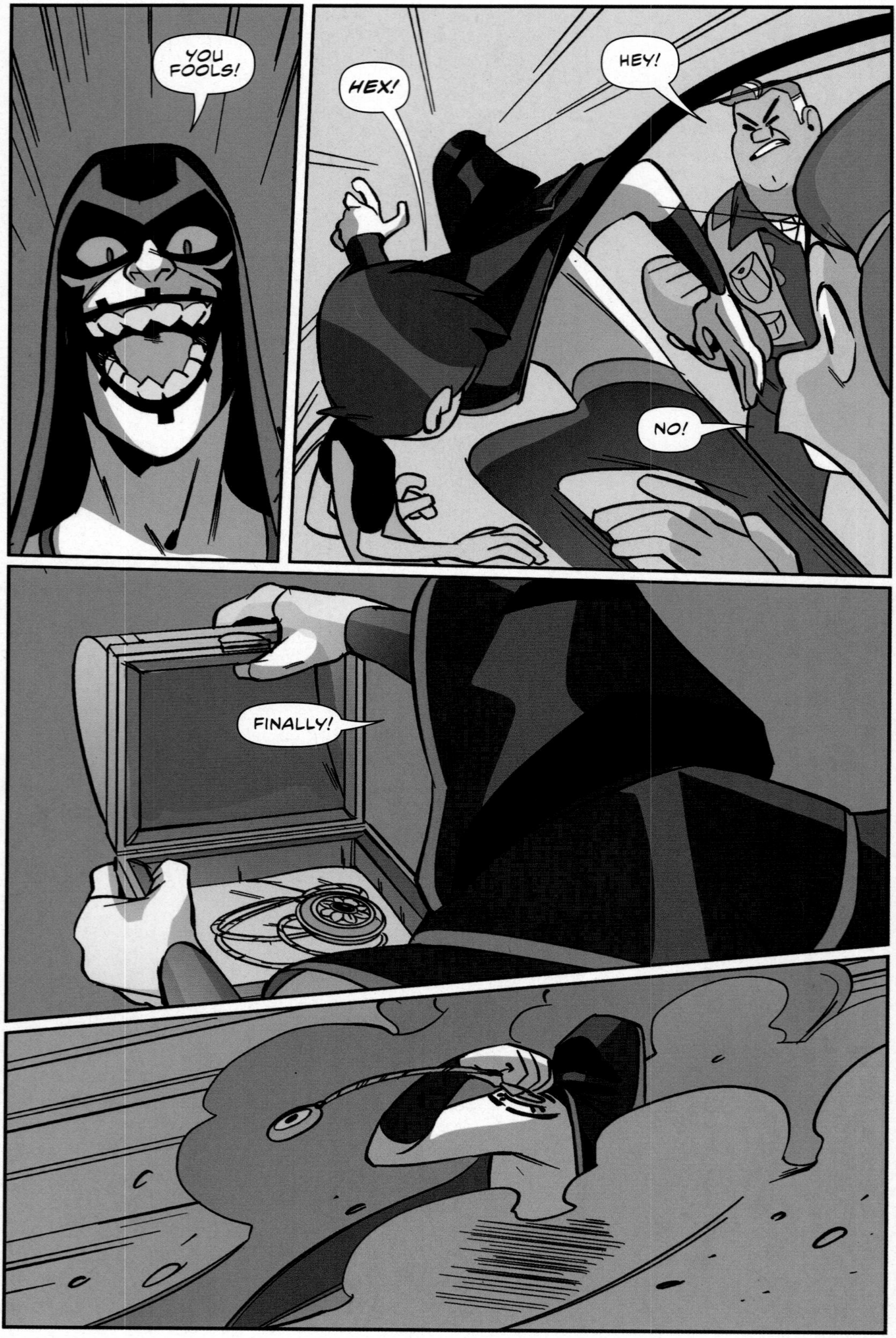
YOU FOOLS!
HEX!
HEY!
NO!
FINALLY!

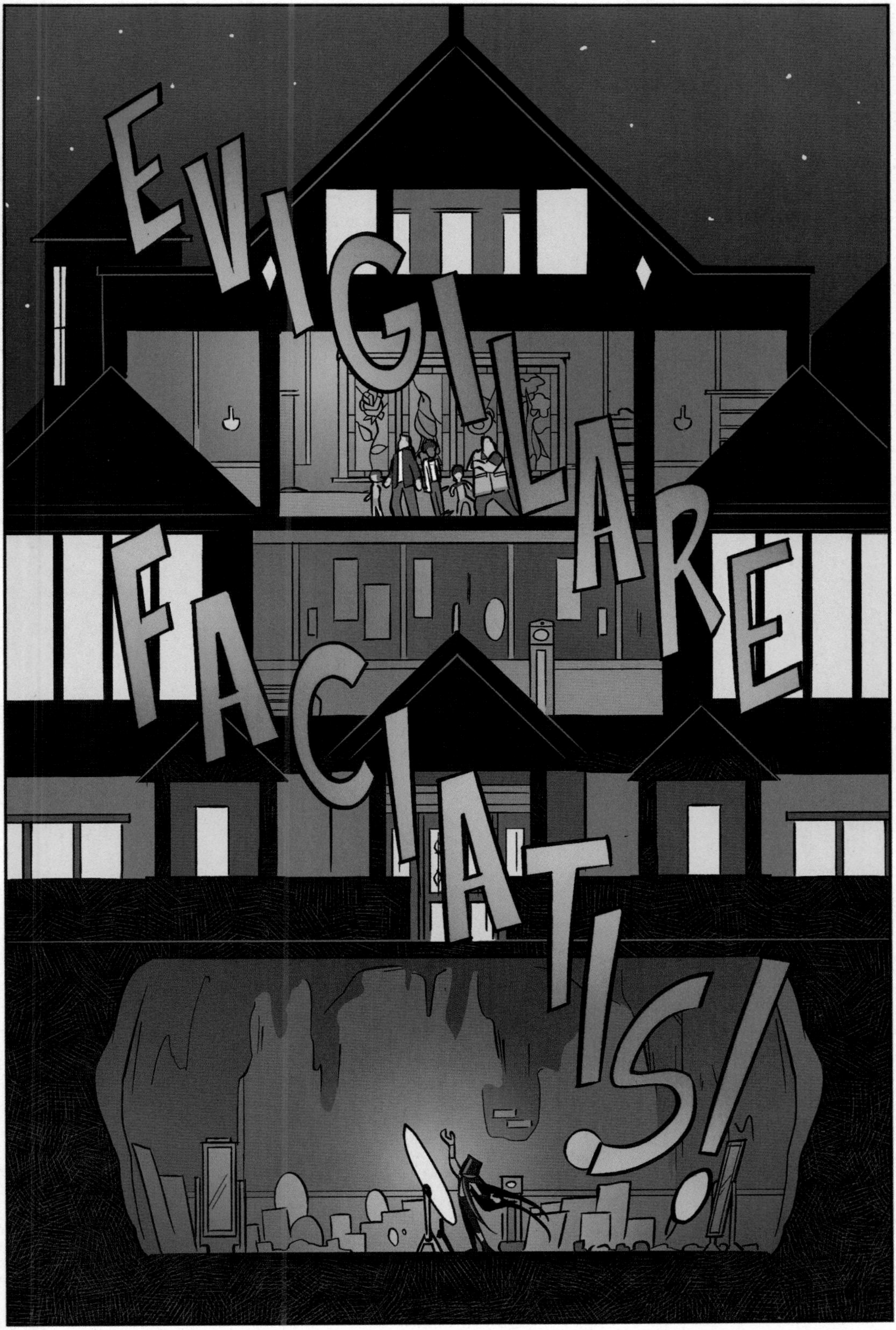
EVIGILARE
FACIATIS!

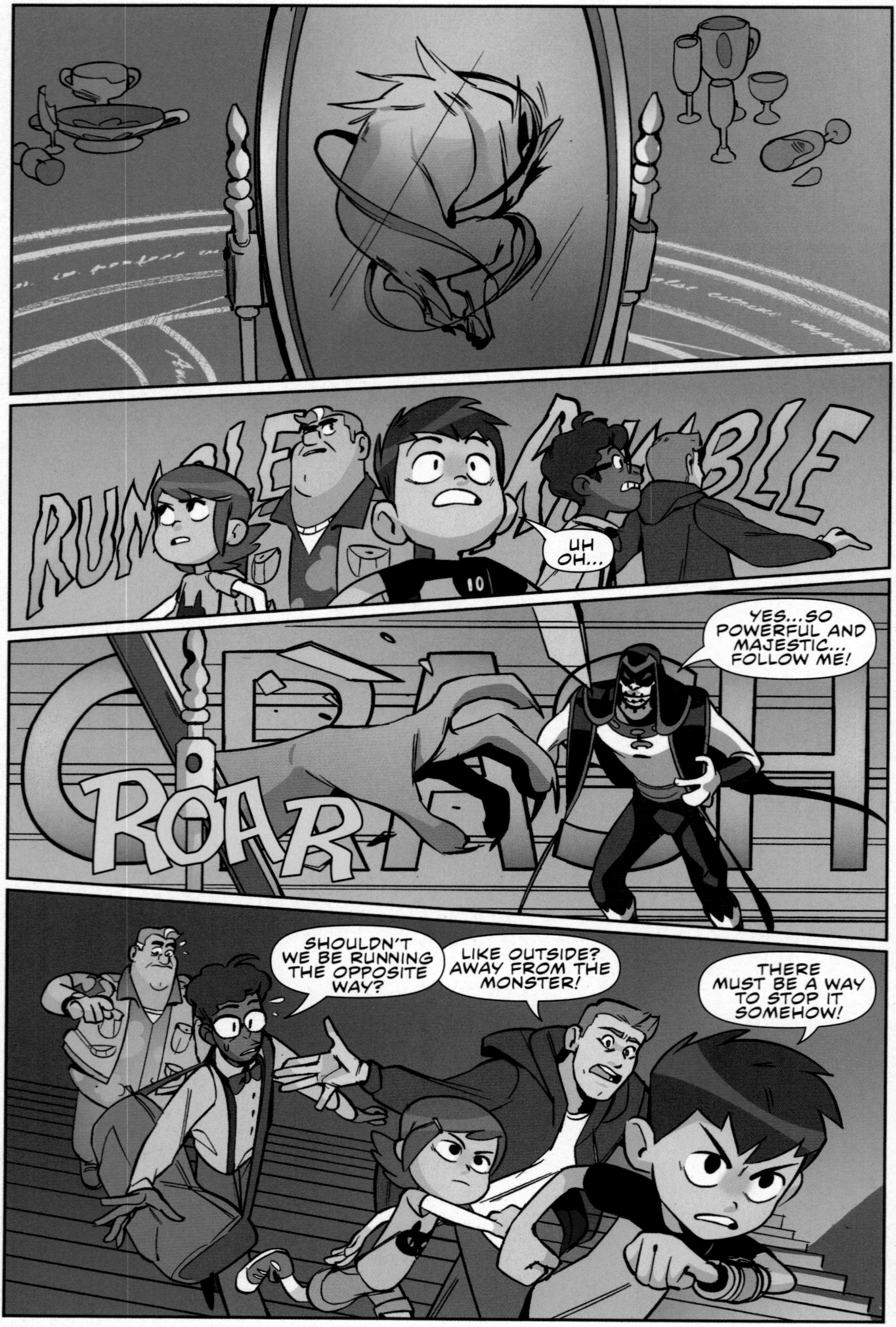
RUMBLE RUMBLE
UH OH...
YES...SO POWERFUL AND MAJESTIC... FOLLOW ME!
CRASH
ROAR
SHOULDN'T WE BE RUNNING THE OPPOSITE WAY?
LIKE OUTSIDE? AWAY FROM THE MONSTER!
THERE MUST BE A WAY TO STOP IT SOMEHOW!

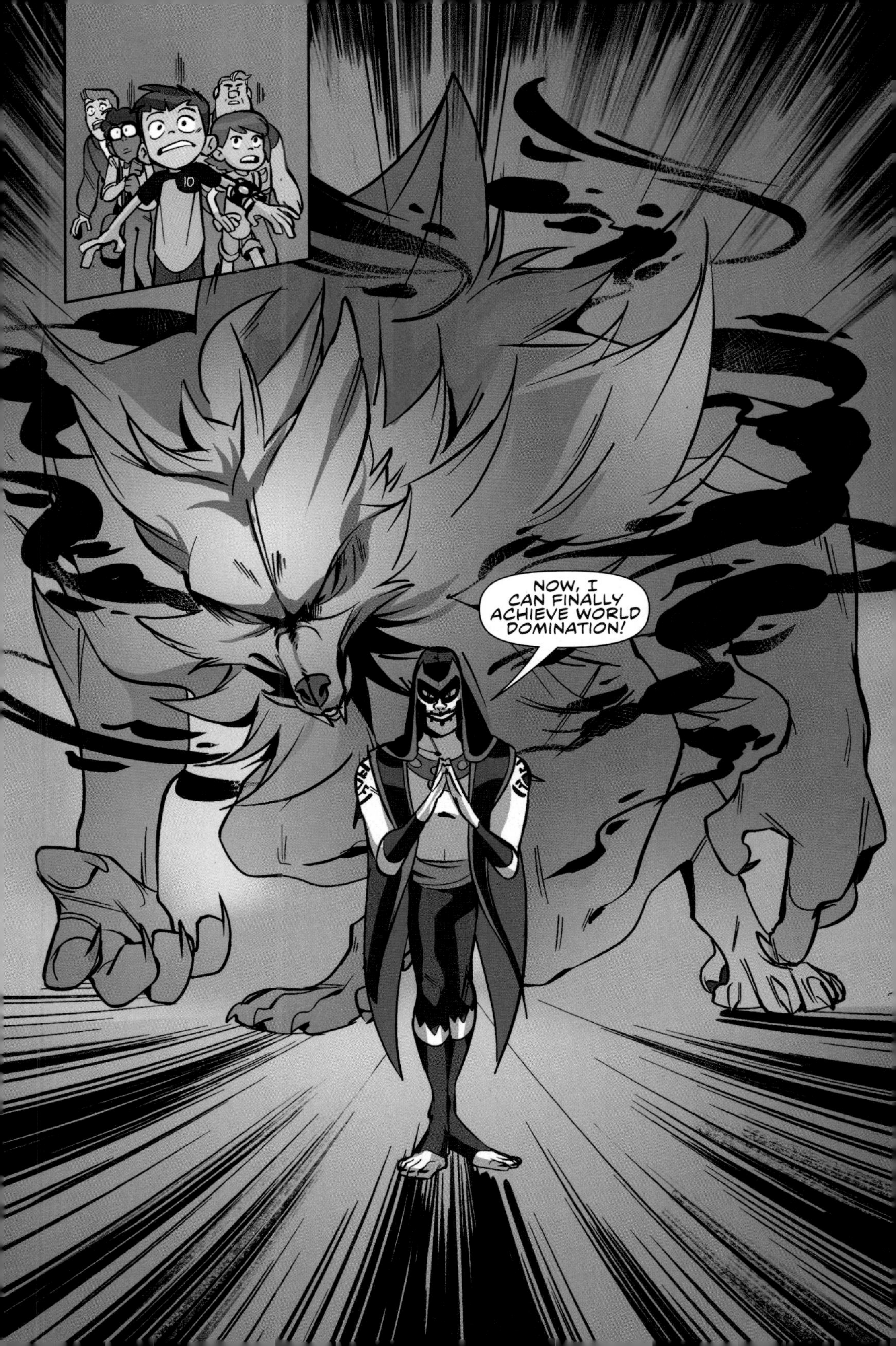
NOW, I CAN FINALLY ACHIEVE WORLD DOMINATION!

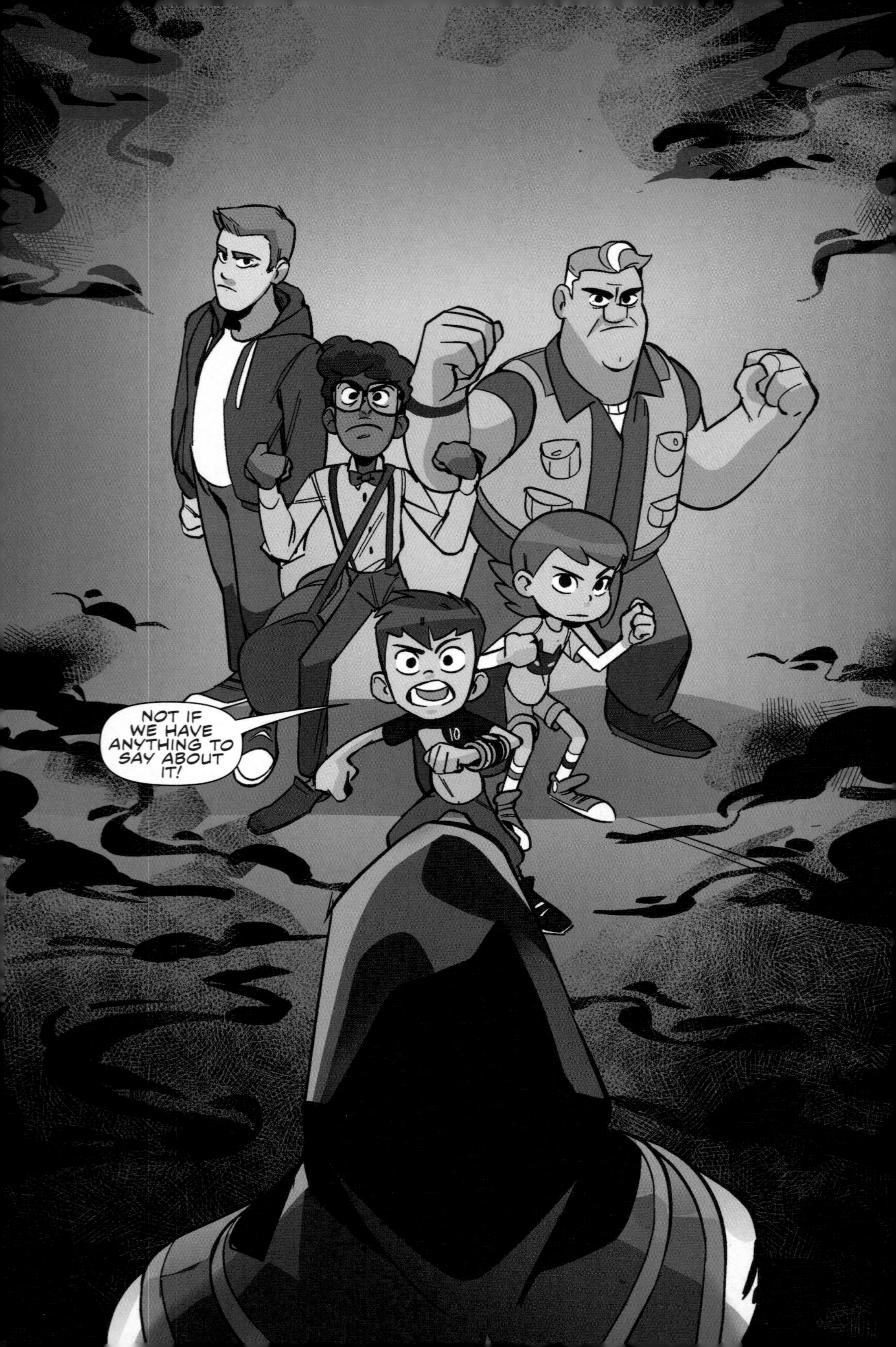
NOT IF WE HAVE ANYTHING TO SAY ABOUT IT!

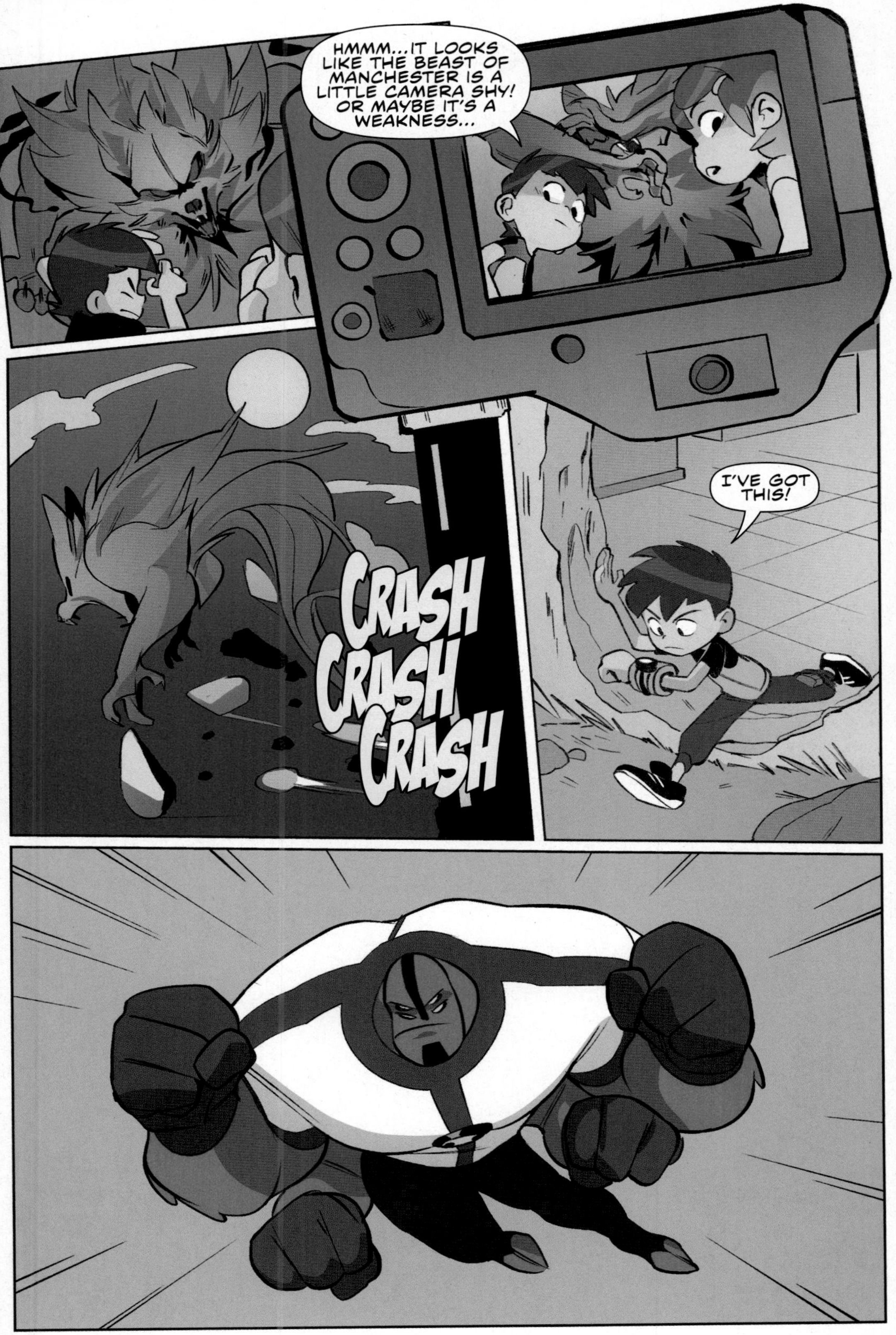
HMMM...IT LOOKS LIKE THE BEAST OF MANCHESTER IS A LITTLE CAMERA SHY! OR MAYBE IT'S A WEAKNESS...
CRASH CRASH CRASH
I'VE GOT THIS!

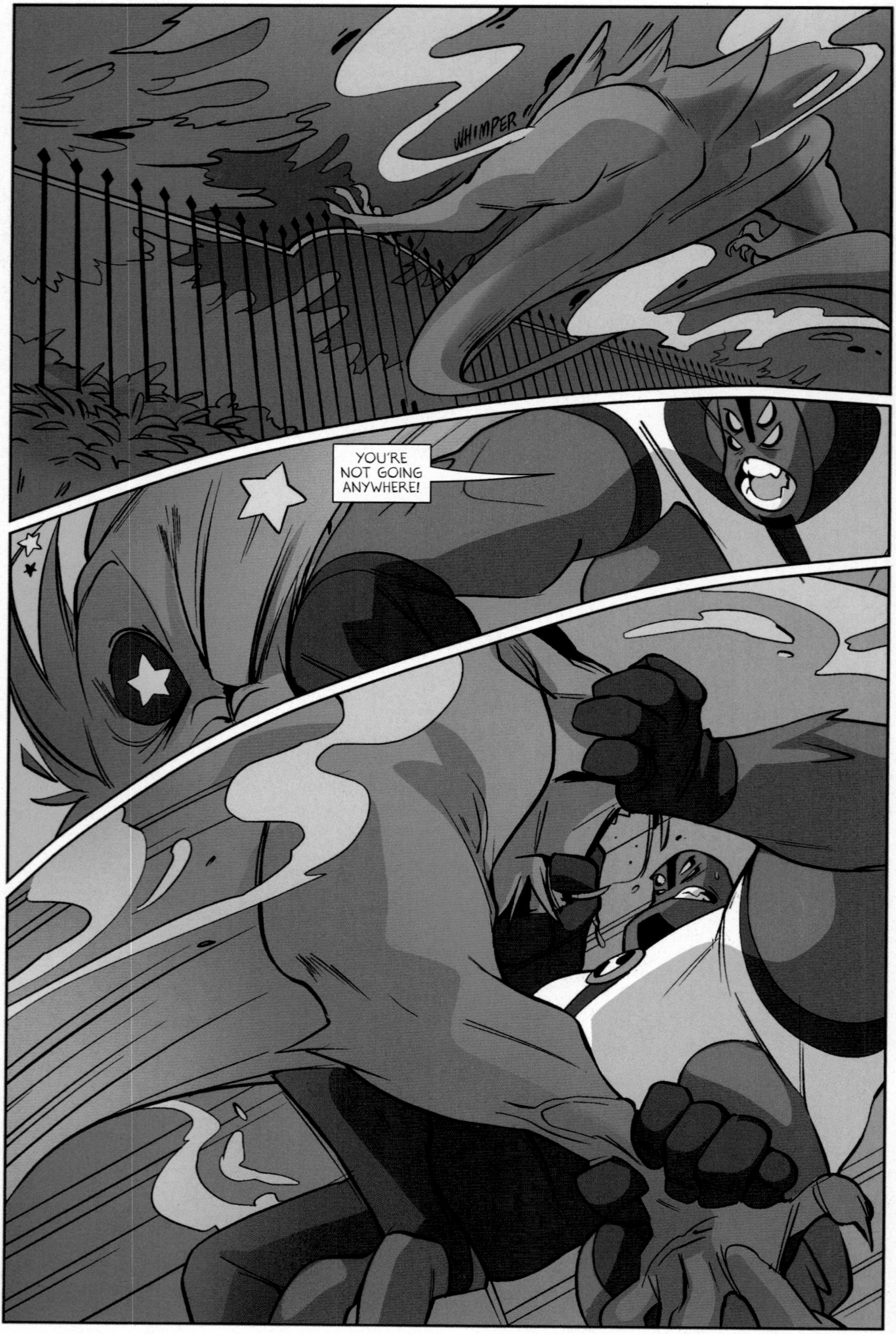
WHIMPER
YOU'RE NOT GOING ANYWHERE!

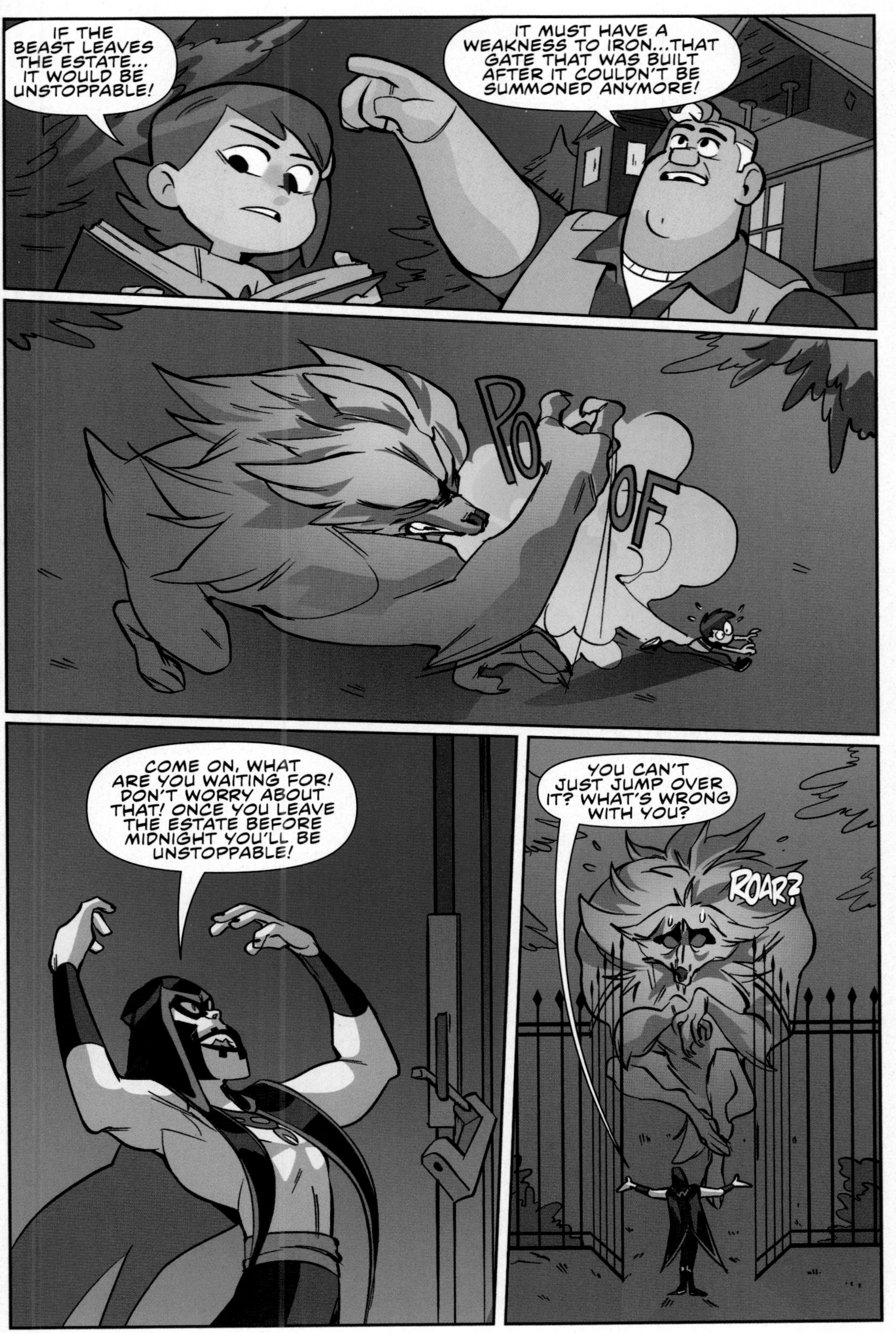
IF THE BEAST LEAVES THE ESTATE... IT WOULD BE UNSTOPPABLE!
IT MUST HAVE A WEAKNESS TO IRON...THAT GATE THAT WAS BUILT AFTER IT COULDN'T BE SUMMONED ANYMORE!
POOF
COME ON, WHAT ARE YOU WAITING FOR! DON'T WORRY ABOUT THAT! ONCE YOU LEAVE THE ESTATE BEFORE MIDNIGHT YOU'LL BE UNSTOPPABLE!
YOU CAN'T JUST JUMP OVER IT? WHAT'S WRONG WITH YOU?
ROAR?

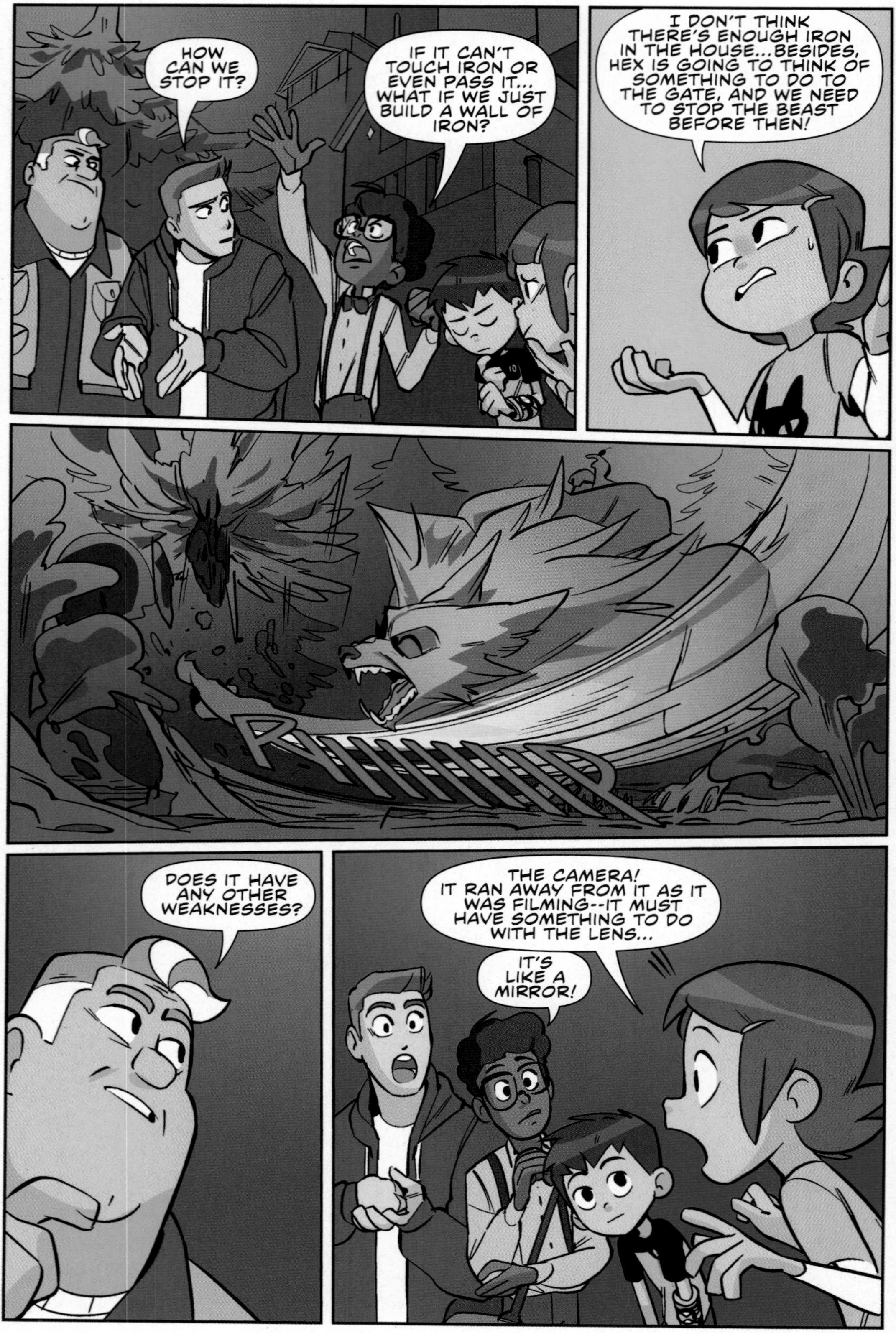
HOW CAN WE STOP IT?
IF IT CAN'T TOUCH IRON OR EVEN PASS IT... WHAT IF WE JUST BUILD A WALL OF IRON?
I DON'T THINK THERE'S ENOUGH IRON IN THE HOUSE...BESIDES, HEX IS GOING TO THINK OF SOMETHING TO DO TO THE GATE, AND WE NEED TO STOP THE BEAST BEFORE THEN!
RHHHR
DOES IT HAVE ANY OTHER WEAKNESSES?
THE CAMERA! IT RAN AWAY FROM IT AS IT WAS FILMING--IT MUST HAVE SOMETHING TO DO WITH THE LENS...
IT'S LIKE A MIRROR!

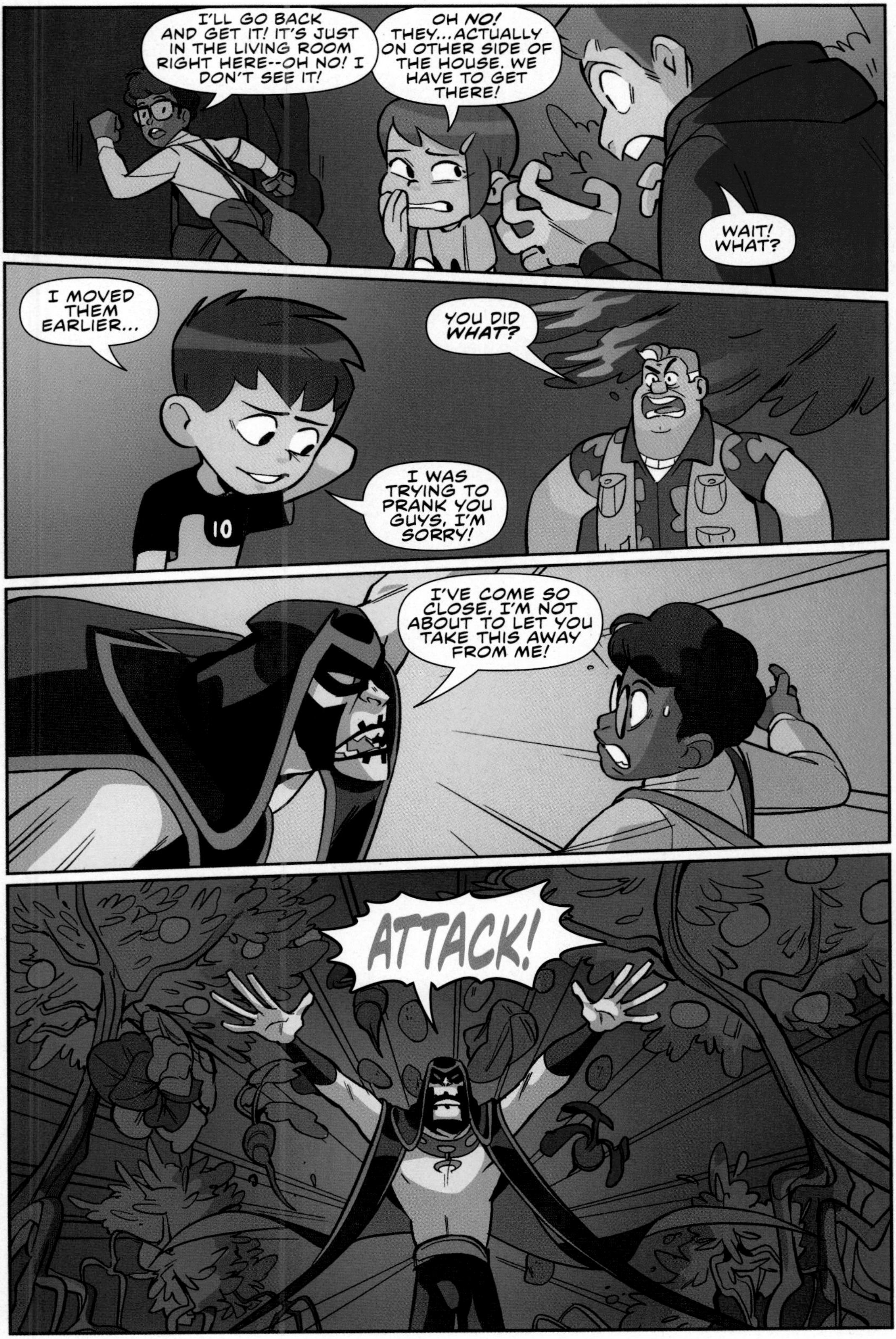
I'LL GO BACK AND GET IT! IT'S JUST IN THE LIVING ROOM RIGHT HERE--OH NO! I DON'T SEE IT!
OH NO! THEY...ACTUALLY ON OTHER SIDE OF THE HOUSE. WE HAVE TO GET THERE!
WAIT! WHAT?
I MOVED THEM EARLIER...
YOU DID WHAT?
I WAS TRYING TO PRANK YOU GUYS, I'M SORRY!
10
I'VE COME SO CLOSE, I'M NOT ABOUT TO LET YOU TAKE THIS AWAY FROM ME!
ATTACK!

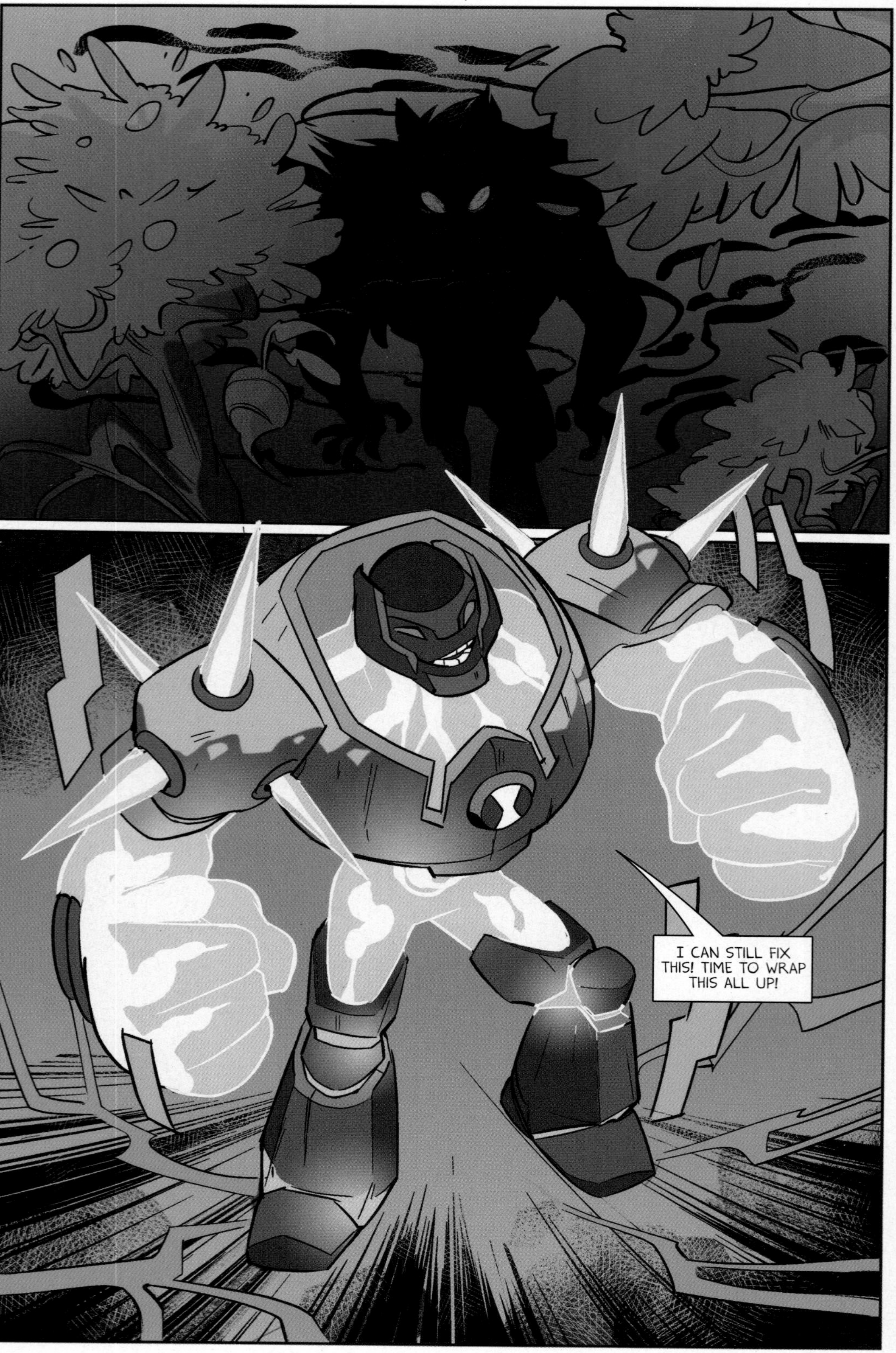
I CAN STILL FIX THIS! TIME TO WRAP THIS ALL UP!

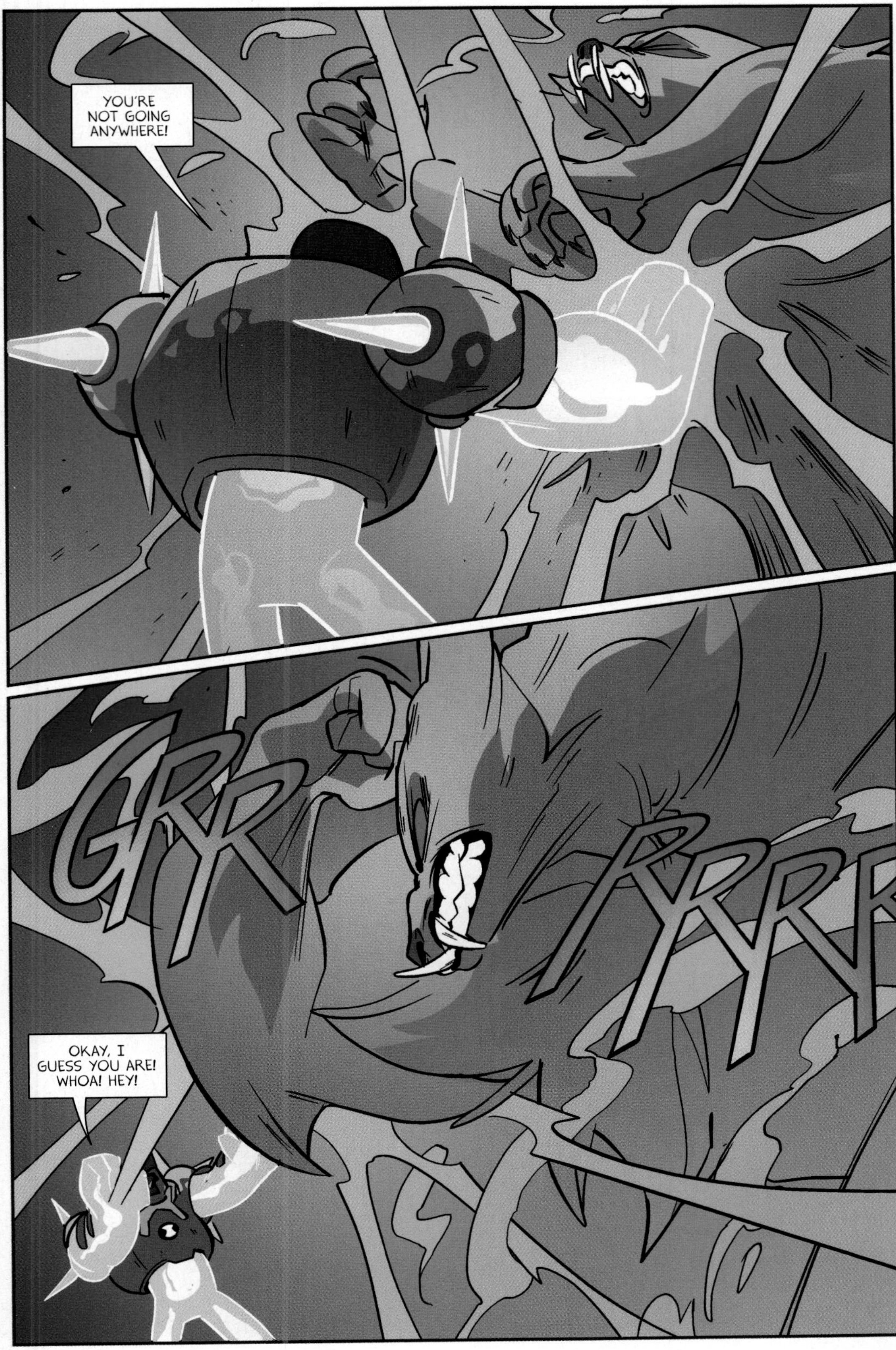
YOU'RE NOT GOING ANYWHERE!
GRRR
RRRRR
OKAY, I GUESS YOU ARE! WHOA! HEY!

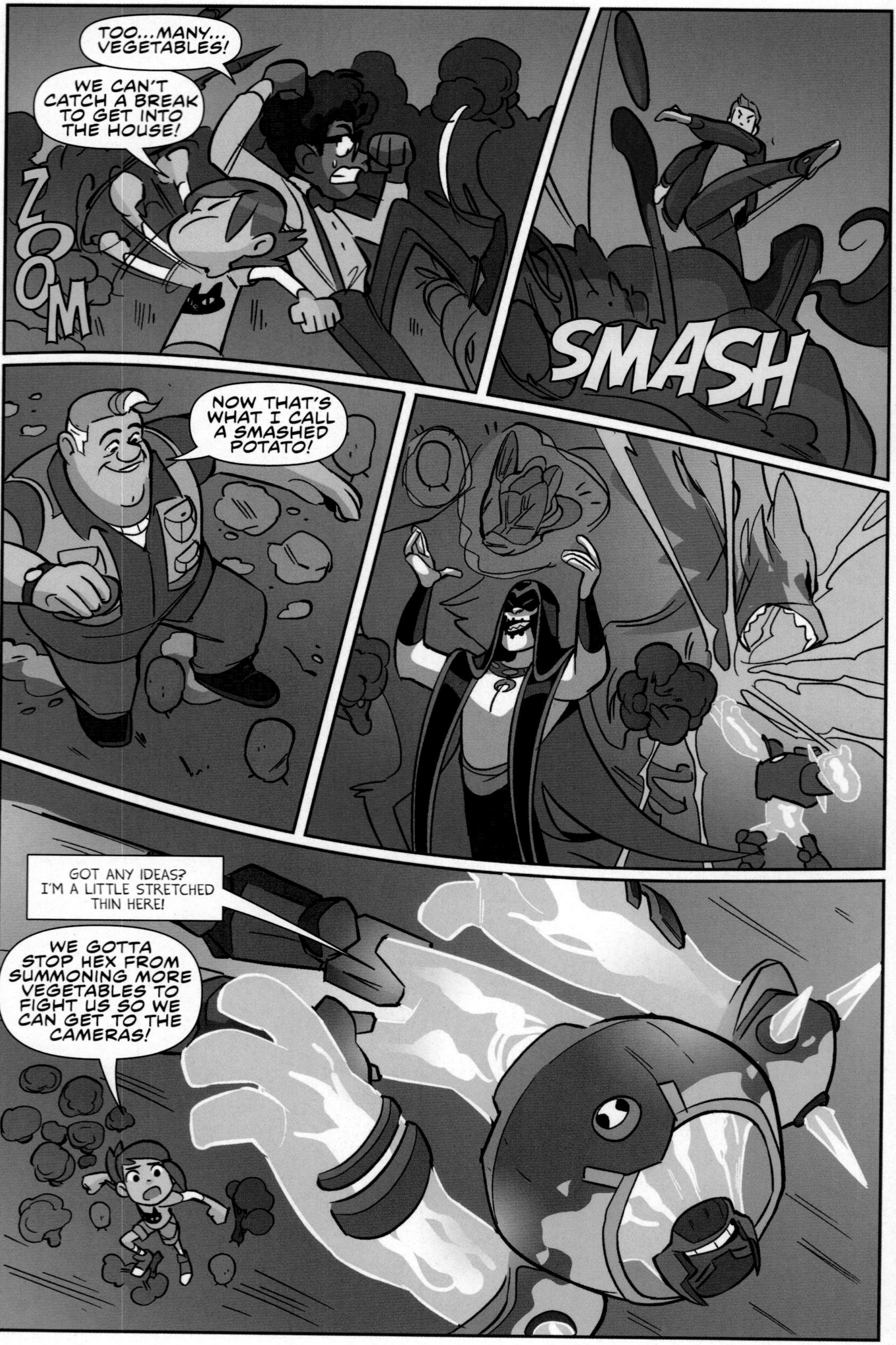
TOO...MANY... VEGETABLES!
WE CAN'T CATCH A BREAK TO GET INTO THE HOUSE!
ZOOM
SMASH
NOW THAT'S WHAT I CALL A SMASHED POTATO!
GOT ANY IDEAS? I'M A LITTLE STRETCHED THIN HERE!
WE GOTTA STOP HEX FROM SUMMONING MORE VEGETABLES TO FIGHT US SO WE CAN GET TO THE CAMERAS!

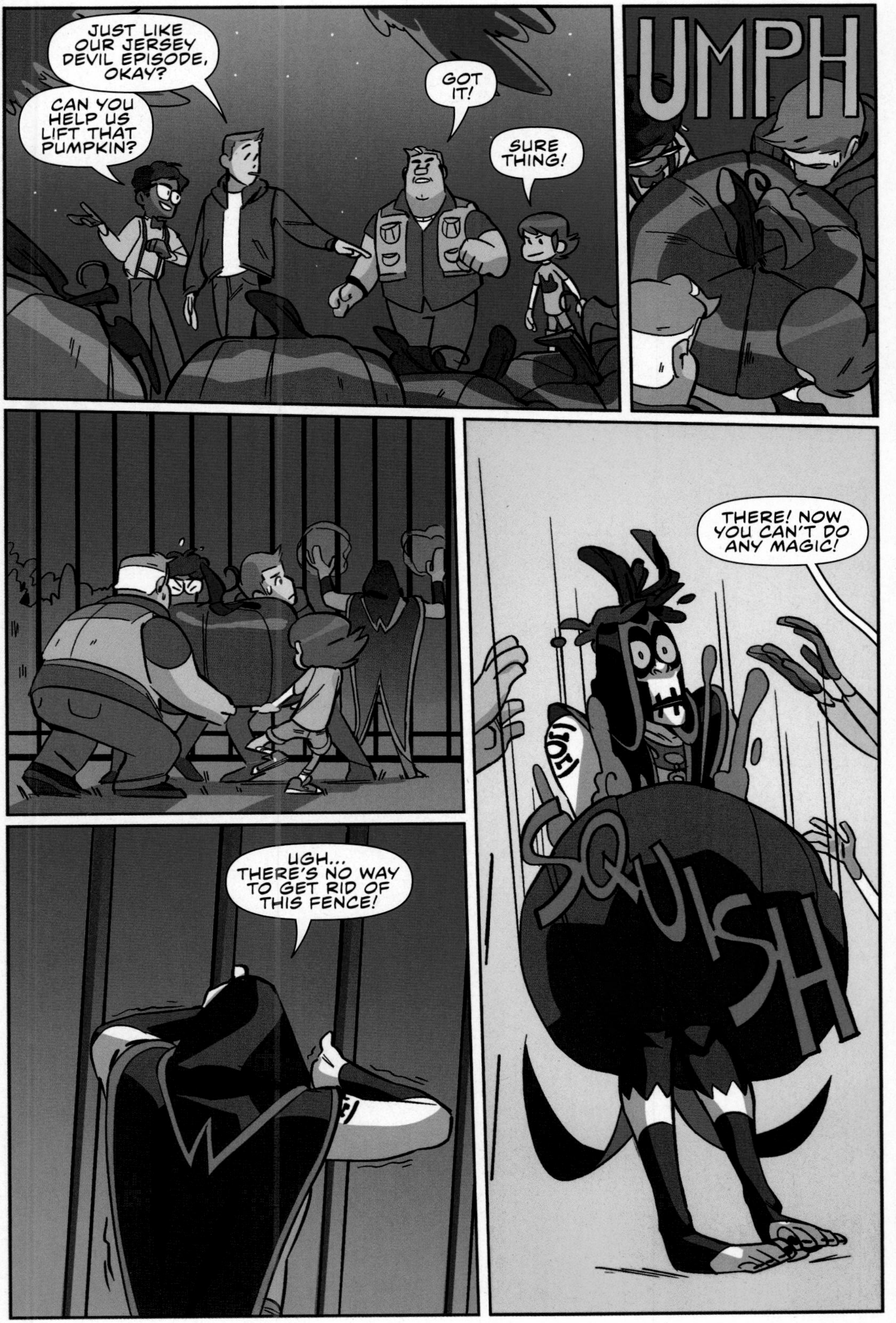
JUST LIKE OUR JERSEY DEVIL EPISODE, OKAY?
CAN YOU HELP US LIFT THAT PUMPKIN?
GOT IT!
SURE THING!
UMPH
THERE! NOW YOU CAN'T DO ANY MAGIC!
SQUISH
UGH... THERE'S NO WAY TO GET RID OF THIS FENCE!

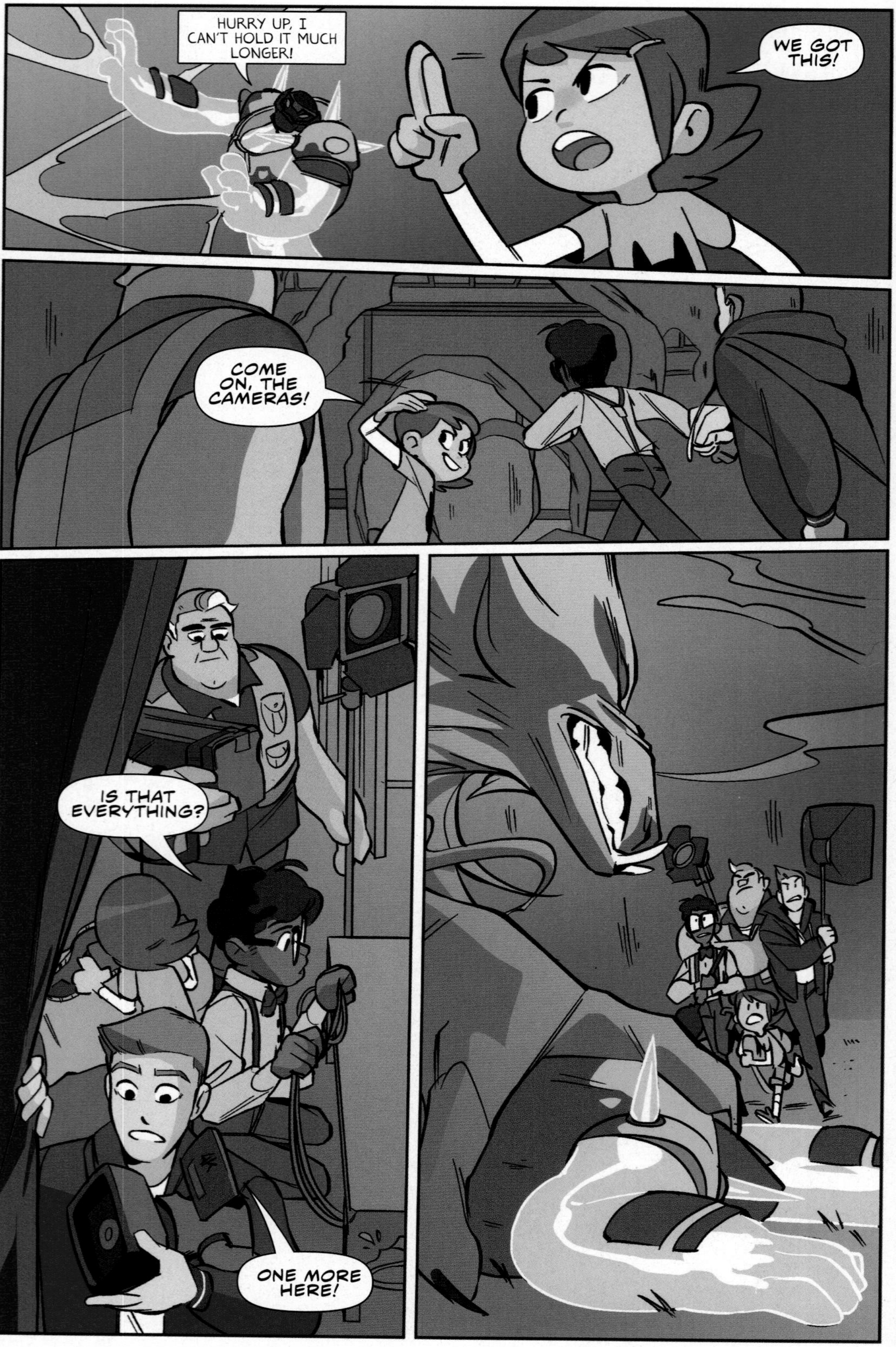
HURRY UP, I CAN'T HOLD IT MUCH LONGER!
WE GOT THIS!
COME ON, THE CAMERAS!
IS THAT EVERYTHING?
ONE MORE HERE!

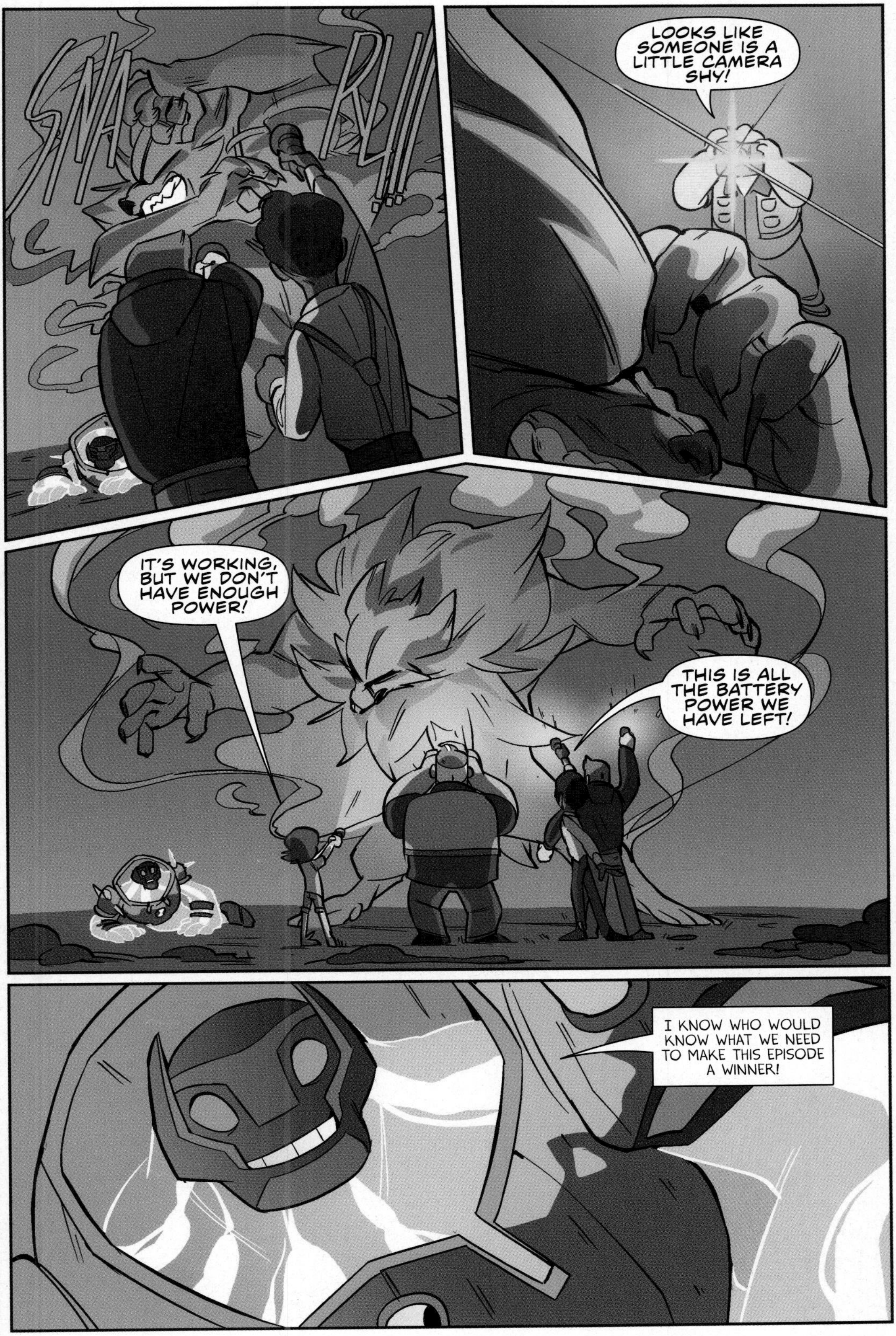
LOOKS LIKE SOMEONE IS A LITTLE CAMERA SHY!
IT'S WORKING, BUT WE DON'T HAVE ENOUGH POWER!
THIS IS ALL THE BATTERY POWER WE HAVE LEFT!
I KNOW WHO WOULD KNOW WHAT WE NEED TO MAKE THIS EPISODE A WINNER!

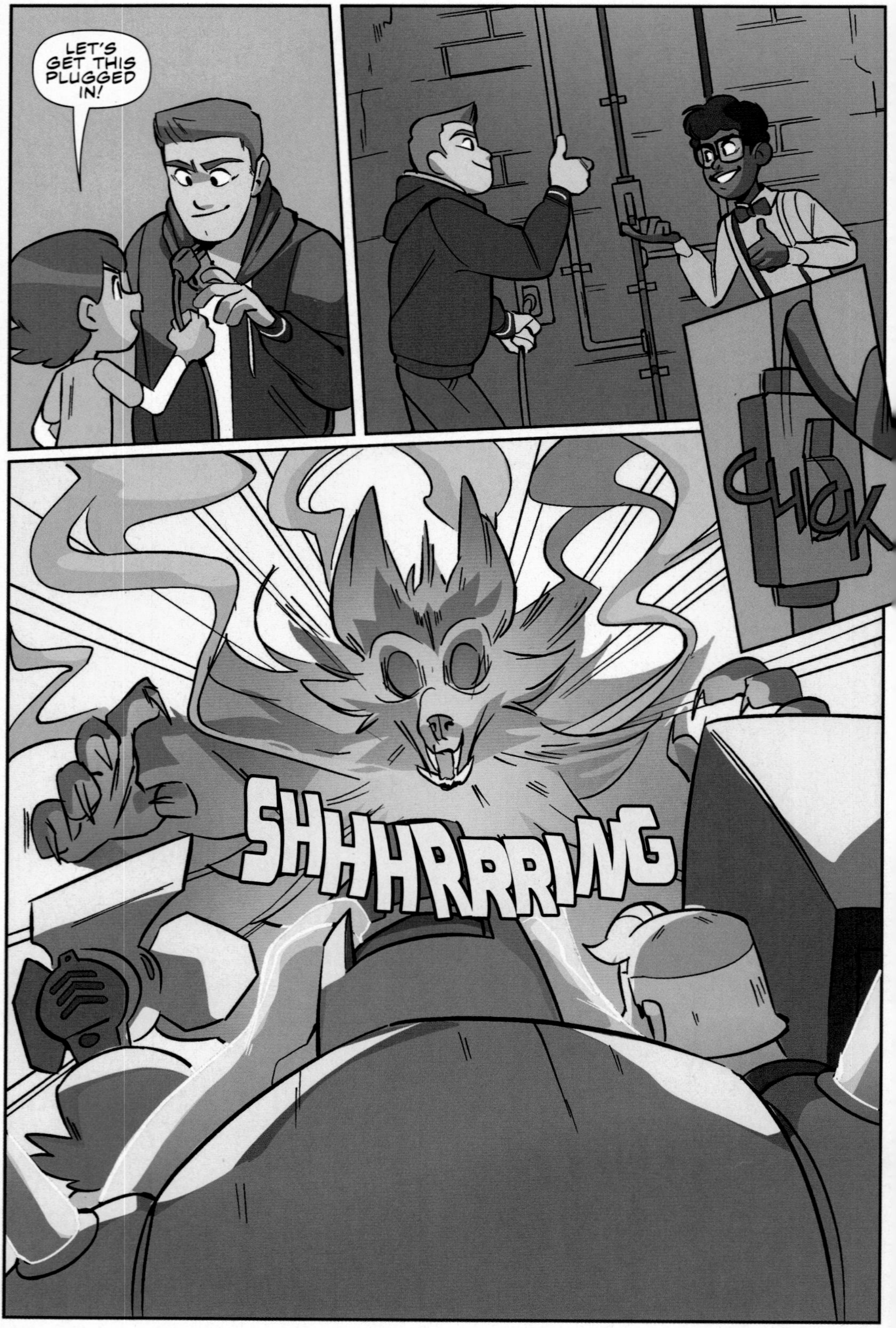
LET'S GET THIS PLUGGED IN!
CHICK
SHHHRRRING

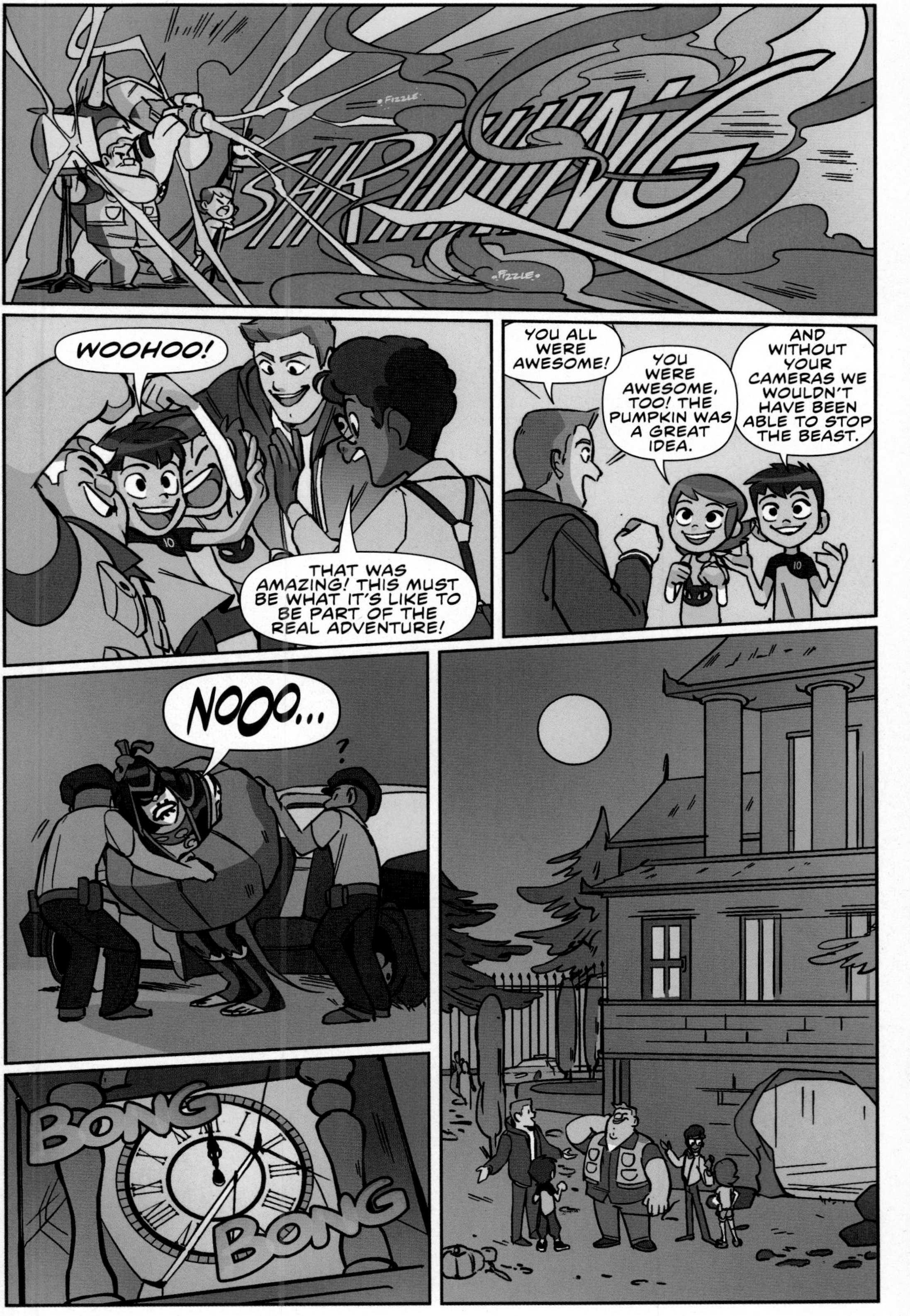
FIZZLE
SHRIIING
FIZZLE
WOOHOO!
THAT WAS AMAZING! THIS MUST BE WHAT IT'S LIKE TO BE PART OF THE REAL ADVENTURE!
YOU ALL WERE AWESOME!
YOU WERE AWESOME, TOO! THE PUMPKIN WAS A GREAT IDEA.
AND WITHOUT YOUR CAMERAS WE WOULDN'T HAVE BEEN ABLE TO STOP THE BEAST.
NOOO...
?
BONG
BONG

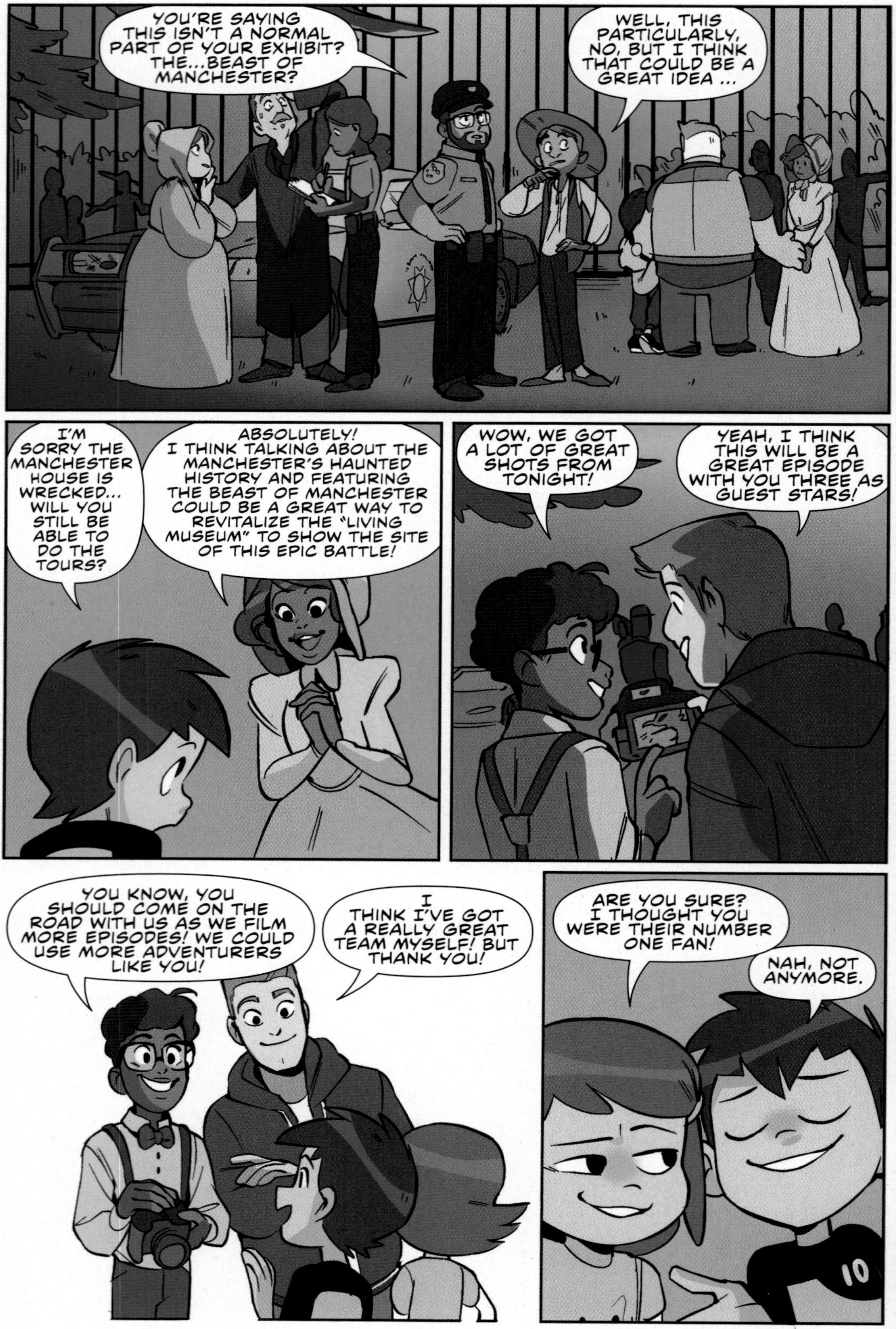
YOU'RE SAYING THIS ISN'T A NORMAL PART OF YOUR EXHIBIT? THE...BEAST OF MANCHESTER?
WELL, THIS PARTICULARLY, NO, BUT I THINK THAT COULD BE A GREAT IDEA ...
I'M SORRY THE MANCHESTER HOUSE IS WRECKED... WILL YOU STILL BE ABLE TO DO THE TOURS?
ABSOLUTELY! I THINK TALKING ABOUT THE MANCHESTER'S HAUNTED HISTORY AND FEATURING THE BEAST OF MANCHESTER COULD BE A GREAT WAY TO REVITALIZE THE "LIVING MUSEUM" TO SHOW THE SITE OF THIS EPIC BATTLE!
WOW, WE GOT A LOT OF GREAT SHOTS FROM TONIGHT!
YEAH, I THINK THIS WILL BE A GREAT EPISODE WITH YOU THREE AS GUEST STARS!
YOU KNOW, YOU SHOULD COME ON THE ROAD WITH US AS WE FILM MORE EPISODES! WE COULD USE MORE ADVENTURERS LIKE YOU!
I THINK I'VE GOT A REALLY GREAT TEAM MYSELF! BUT THANK YOU!
ARE YOU SURE? I THOUGHT YOU WERE THEIR NUMBER ONE FAN!
NAH, NOT ANYMORE.
10

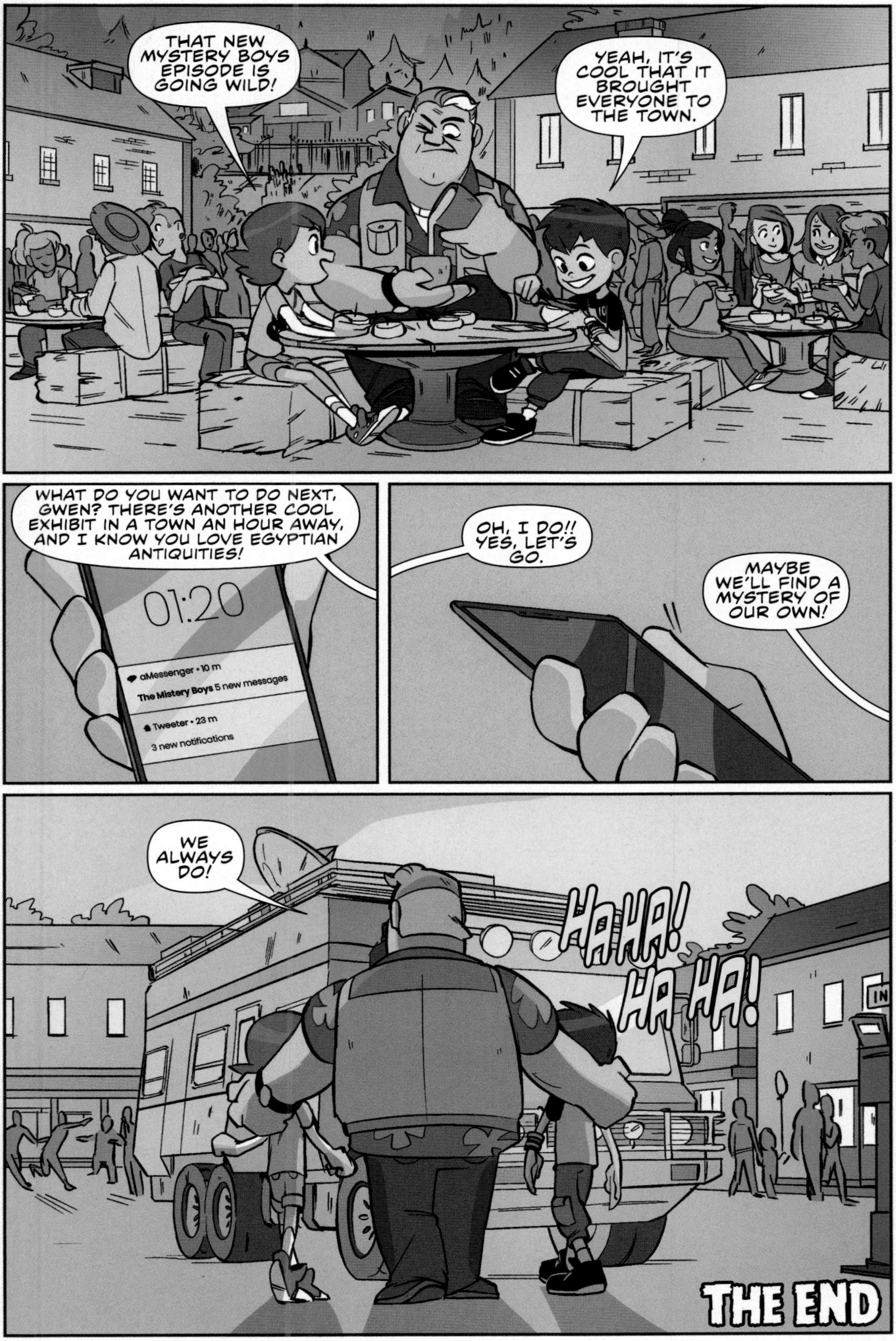
THAT NEW MYSTERY BOYS EPISODE IS GOING WILD!
YEAH, IT'S COOL THAT IT BROUGHT EVERYONE TO THE TOWN.
WHAT DO YOU WANT TO DO NEXT, GWEN? THERE'S ANOTHER COOL EXHIBIT IN A TOWN AN HOUR AWAY, AND I KNOW YOU LOVE EGYPTIAN ANTIQUITIES!
01:20
aMessenger • 10 m
The Mistery Boys 5 new messages
Tweeter • 23 m
3 new notifications
OH, I DO!! YES, LET'S GO.
MAYBE WE'LL FIND A MYSTERY OF OUR OWN!
WE ALWAYS DO!
HA HA!
HA HA!
THE END

BEN'S ADVENTURES IN THE RUSTBUCKET CONTINUE IN...

"THE CREATURE FROM SERENITY SHORE"

AVAILABLE FALL 2020

CN
BEN 10
THE CREATURE FROM SERENITY SHORE
BEN 10
THE CREATURE FROM SERENITY SHORE
C.B. LEE
MATTIA DI MEO

WRITTEN BY
C.B. LEE

ILLUSTRATED BY
MATTIA DI MEO

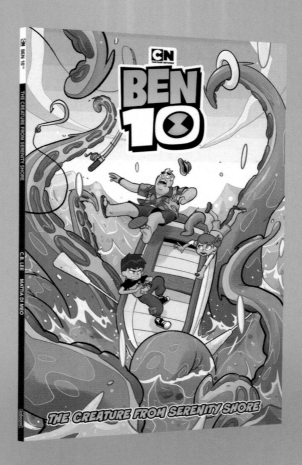

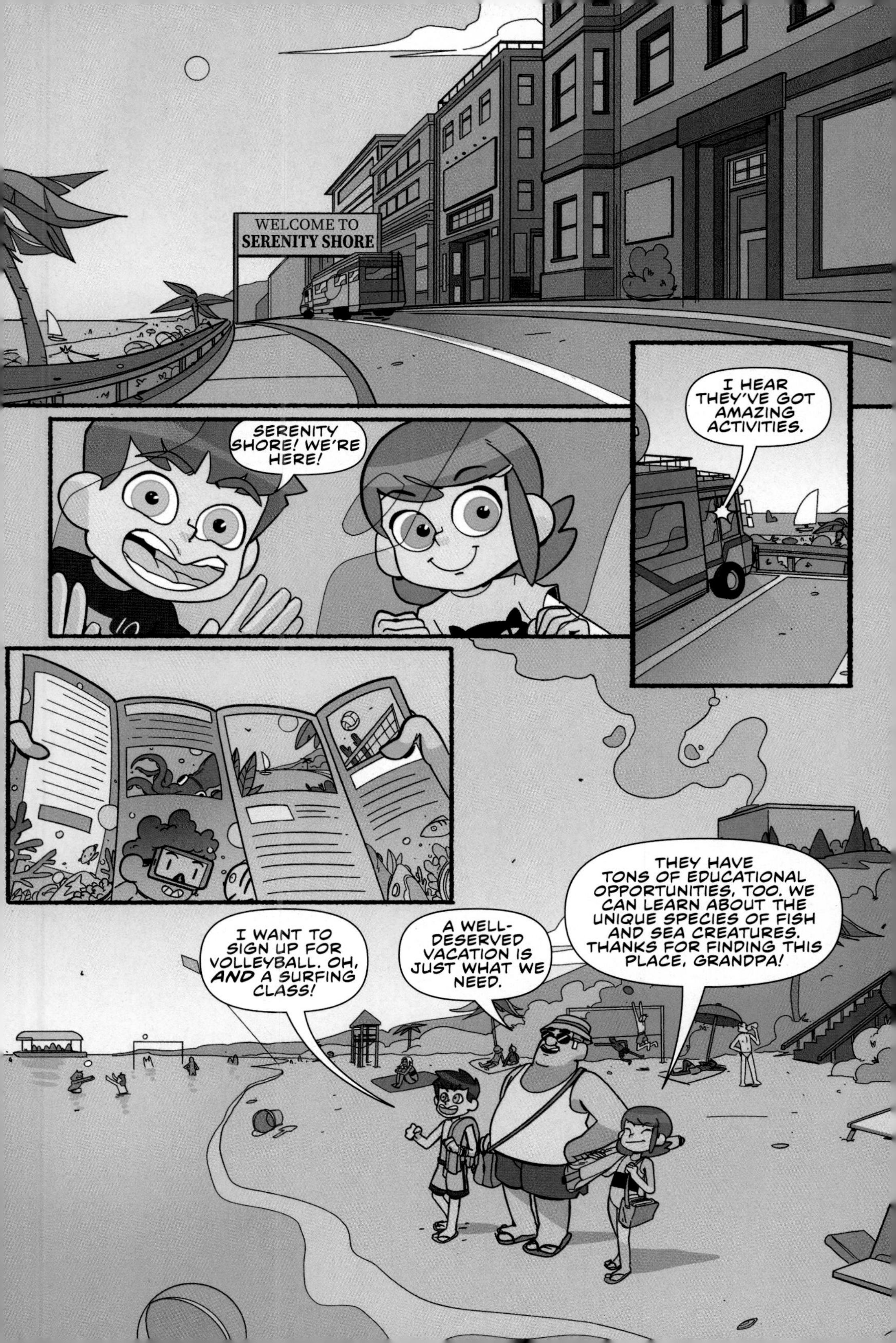
WELCOME TO
SERENITY SHORE
SERENITY SHORE! WE'RE HERE!
I HEAR THEY'VE GOT AMAZING ACTIVITIES.
I WANT TO SIGN UP FOR VOLLEYBALL. OH, AND A SURFING CLASS!
A WELL-DESERVED VACATION IS JUST WHAT WE NEED.
THEY HAVE TONS OF EDUCATIONAL OPPORTUNITIES, TOO. WE CAN LEARN ABOUT THE UNIQUE SPECIES OF FISH AND SEA CREATURES. THANKS FOR FINDING THIS PLACE, GRANDPA!

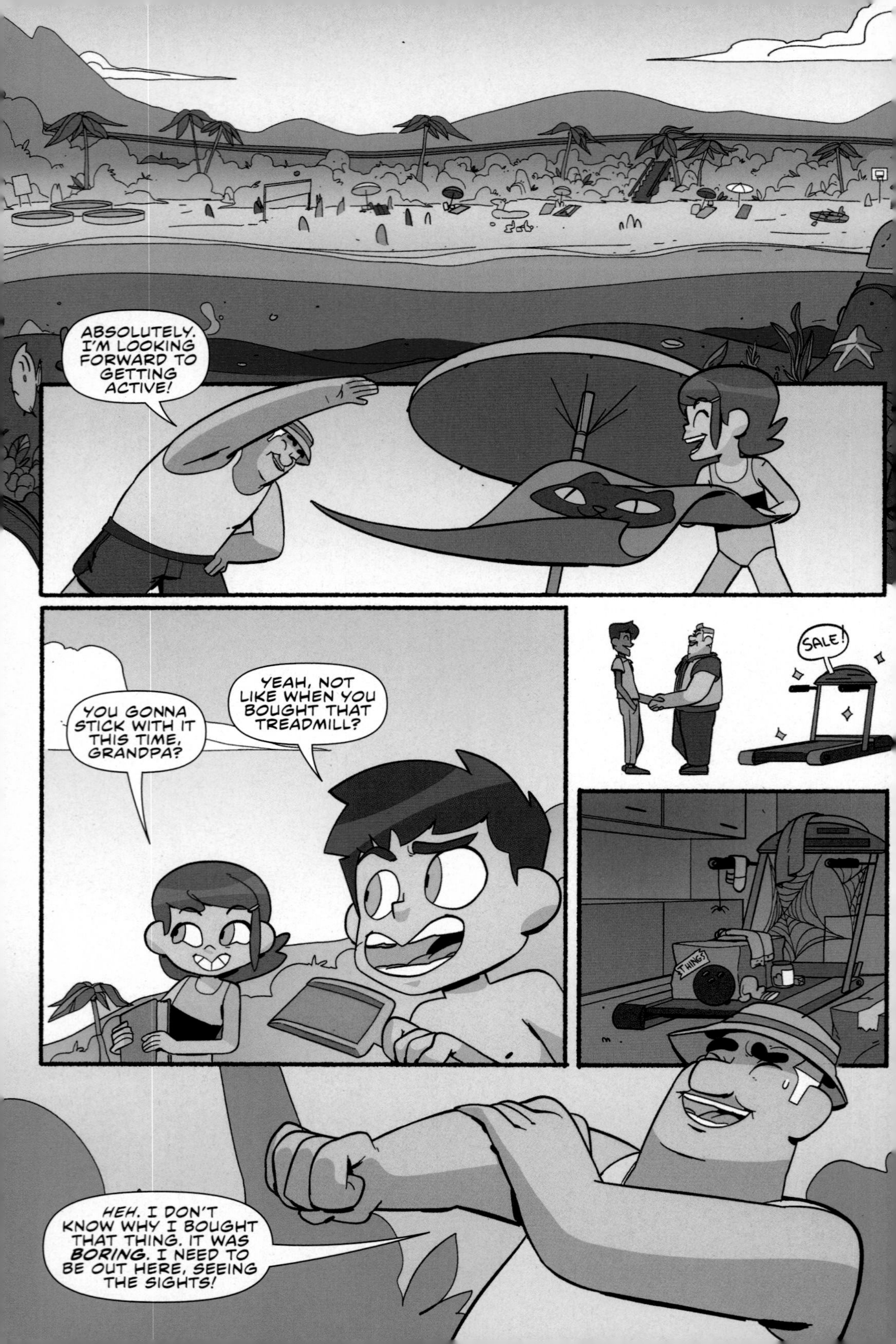
ABSOLUTELY. I'M LOOKING FORWARD TO GETTING ACTIVE!
YOU GONNA STICK WITH IT THIS TIME, GRANDPA?
YEAH, NOT LIKE WHEN YOU BOUGHT THAT TREADMILL?
SALE!
THINGS
HEH. I DON'T KNOW WHY I BOUGHT THAT THING. IT WAS BORING. I NEED TO BE OUT HERE, SEEING THE SIGHTS!

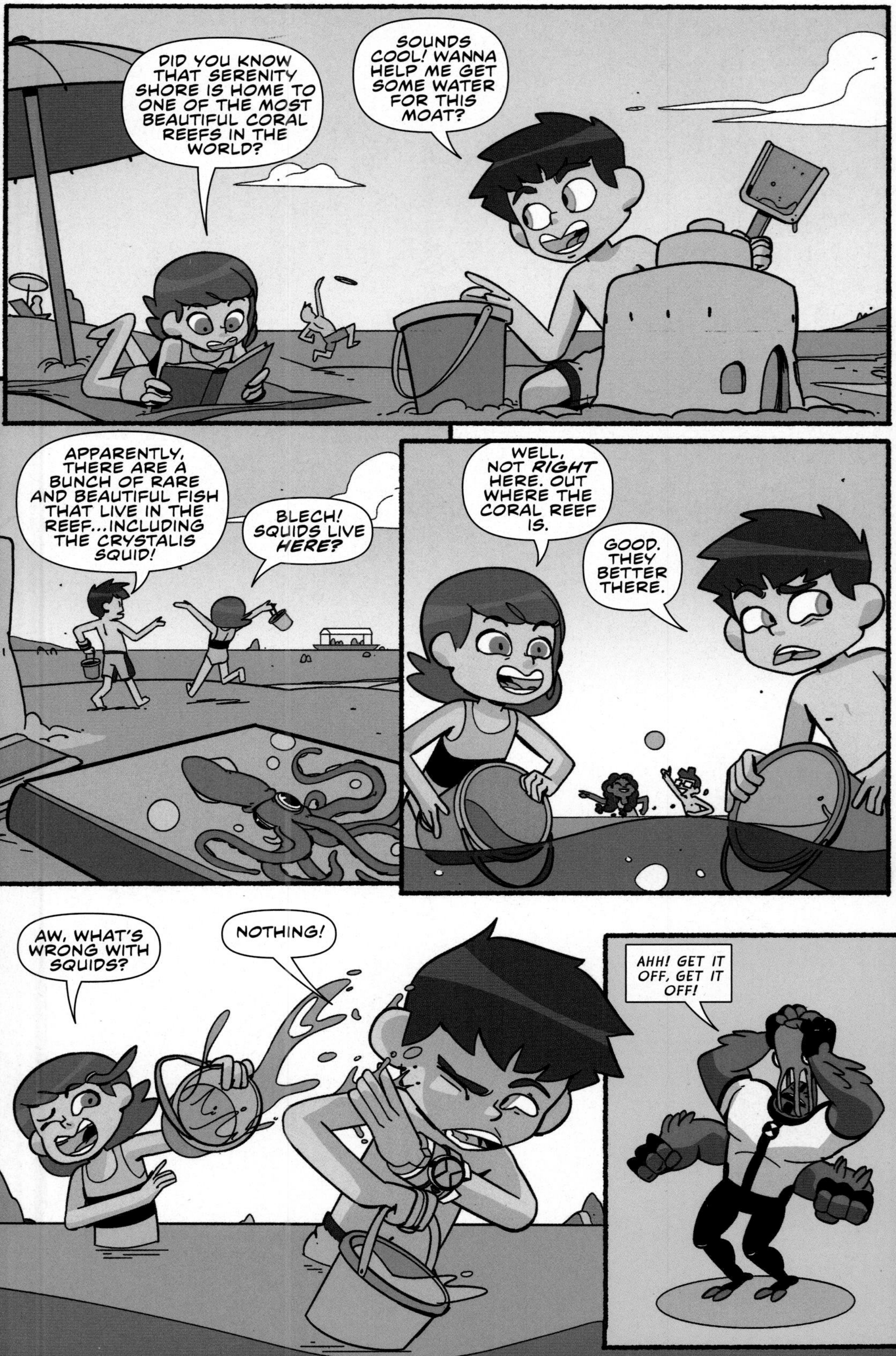
DID YOU KNOW THAT SERENITY SHORE IS HOME TO ONE OF THE MOST BEAUTIFUL CORAL REEFS IN THE WORLD?
SOUNDS COOL! WANNA HELP ME GET SOME WATER FOR THIS MOAT?
APPARENTLY, THERE ARE A BUNCH OF RARE AND BEAUTIFUL FISH THAT LIVE IN THE REEF...INCLUDING THE CRYSTALIS SQUID!
BLECH! SQUIDS LIVE *HERE?*
WELL, NOT *RIGHT* HERE. OUT WHERE THE CORAL REEF IS.
GOOD. THEY BETTER THERE.
AW, WHAT'S WRONG WITH SQUIDS?
NOTHING!
AHH! GET IT OFF, GET IT OFF!

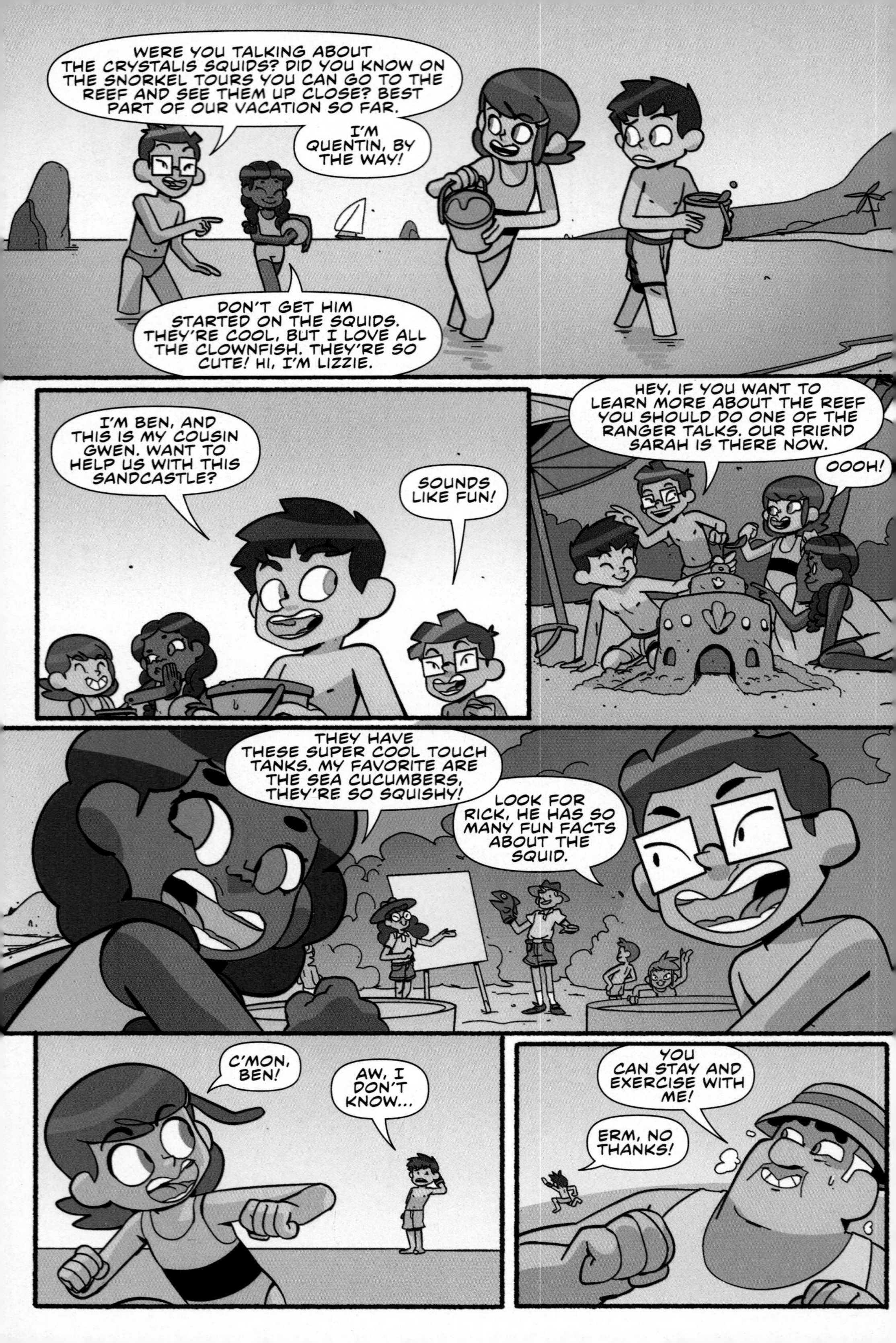
WERE YOU TALKING ABOUT THE CRYSTALIS SQUIDS? DID YOU KNOW ON THE SNORKEL TOURS YOU CAN GO TO THE REEF AND SEE THEM UP CLOSE? BEST PART OF OUR VACATION SO FAR.
I'M QUENTIN, BY THE WAY!
DON'T GET HIM STARTED ON THE SQUIDS. THEY'RE COOL, BUT I LOVE ALL THE CLOWNFISH. THEY'RE SO CUTE! HI, I'M LIZZIE.
I'M BEN, AND THIS IS MY COUSIN GWEN. WANT TO HELP US WITH THIS SANDCASTLE?
SOUNDS LIKE FUN!
HEY, IF YOU WANT TO LEARN MORE ABOUT THE REEF YOU SHOULD DO ONE OF THE RANGER TALKS. OUR FRIEND SARAH IS THERE NOW.
OOOH!
THEY HAVE THESE SUPER COOL TOUCH TANKS. MY FAVORITE ARE THE SEA CUCUMBERS, THEY'RE SO SQUISHY!
LOOK FOR RICK, HE HAS SO MANY FUN FACTS ABOUT THE SQUID.
C'MON, BEN!
AW, I DON'T KNOW...
YOU CAN STAY AND EXERCISE WITH ME!
ERM, NO THANKS!

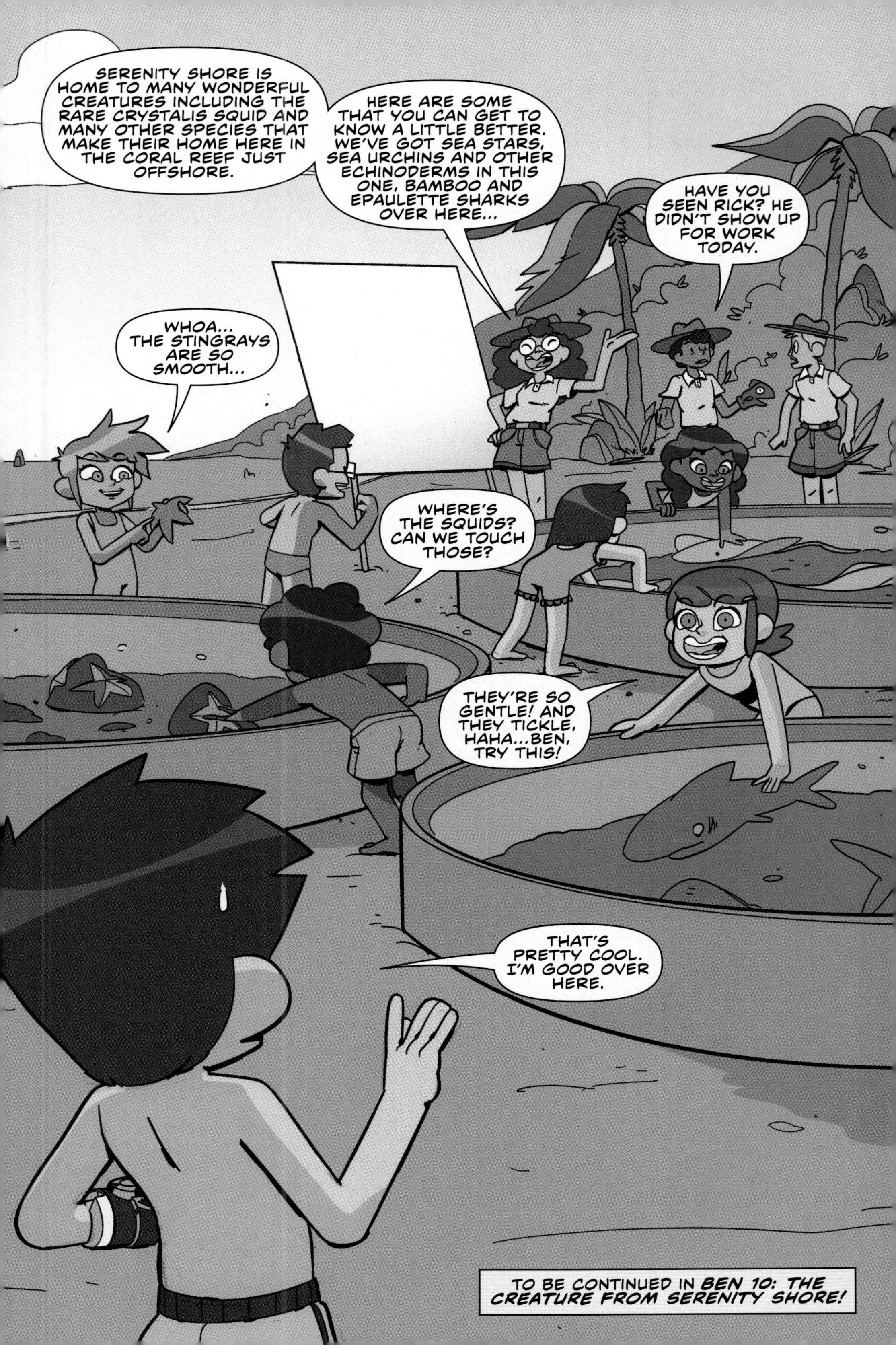
SERENITY SHORE IS HOME TO MANY WONDERFUL CREATURES INCLUDING THE RARE CRYSTALIS SQUID AND MANY OTHER SPECIES THAT MAKE THEIR HOME HERE IN THE CORAL REEF JUST OFFSHORE.
HERE ARE SOME THAT YOU CAN GET TO KNOW A LITTLE BETTER. WE'VE GOT SEA STARS, SEA URCHINS AND OTHER ECHINODERMS IN THIS ONE, BAMBOO AND EPAULETTE SHARKS OVER HERE...
HAVE YOU SEEN RICK? HE DIDN'T SHOW UP FOR WORK TODAY.
WHOA... THE STINGRAYS ARE SO SMOOTH...
WHERE'S THE SQUIDS? CAN WE TOUCH THOSE?
THEY'RE SO GENTLE! AND THEY TICKLE, HAHA...BEN, TRY THIS!
THAT'S PRETTY COOL. I'M GOOD OVER HERE.
TO BE CONTINUED IN *BEN 10: THE CREATURE FROM SERENITY SHORE!*

DISCOVER
EXPLOSIVE NEW WORLDS

ADVENTURE TIME

BRAVE CHEF BRIANNA

KELLY THOMPSON
BRIANNE DROUHARD
M. VICTORIA ROBADO
MEGA PRINCESS

THE NOT-SO SECRET SOCIETY
DALEY · CRAFTS · CLARK · BRUNI
KEEP OUT
CAUTION

OVER THE GARDEN WALL

STEVEN UNIVERSE
VOLUME ONE

kaboom!

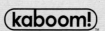

AVAILABLE AT YOUR LOCAL COMICS SHOP AND BOOKSTORE

To find a comics shop in your area, visit www.comicshoplocator.com

WWW.**BOOM-STUDIOS**.COM

Adventure Time
Pendleton Ward and Others
Volume 1
ISBN: 978-1-60886-280-1 | $14.99 US
Volume 2
ISBN: 978-1-60886-323-5 | $14.99 US
Adventure Time: Islands
ISBN: 978-1-60886-972-5 | $9.99 US

The Amazing World of Gumball
Ben Bocquelet and Others
Volume 1
ISBN: 978-1-60886-488-1 | $14.99 US
Volume 2
ISBN: 978-1-60886-793-6 | $14.99 US

Brave Chef Brianna
Sam Sykes, Selina Espiritu
ISBN: 978-1-68415-050-2 | $14.99 US

Mega Princess
Kelly Thompson, Brianne Drouhard
ISBN: 978-1-68415-007-6 | $14.99 US

The Not-So Secret Society
Matthew Daley, Arlene Daley, Wook Jin Clark
ISBN: 978-1-60886-997-8 | $9.99 US

Over the Garden Wall
Patrick McHale, Jim Campbell and Others
Volume 1
ISBN: 978-1-60886-940-4 | $14.99 US
Volume 2
ISBN: 978-1-68415-006-9 | $14.99 US

Steven Universe
Rebecca Sugar and Others
Volume 1
ISBN: 978-1-60886-706-6 | $14.99 US
Volume 2
ISBN: 978-1-60886-796-7 | $14.99 US

Steven Universe & The Crystal Gems
ISBN: 978-1-60886-921-3 | $14.99 US

Steven Universe: Too Cool for School
ISBN: 978-1-60886-771-4 | $14.99 US